how the mind breaks

A DARK ROMANCE

USA TODAY BESTSELLING AUTHOR

DANI RENÉ

Copyright © 2020 by Dani René
Published by Dani René
Cover Design by Marisa Shor, Cover Me Darling
Edited by Candice Royer
Proofed by Michelle Myers

All rights reserved, including the right to reproduce this book or portions thereof in any form whatsoever.
The following story contains mature themes, strong language, and sexual situations. It is intended for adult readers.
No part of this book may be reproduced or transmitted in any form or by any means, electronic or mechanical, including photocopying, recording, or by any information storage and retrieval system, without permission in writing. If you would like to share this book with another person, please purchase an additional copy for each recipient. If you're reading this book and did not purchase it, or it was not purchased for your enjoyment only, then please purchase your own copy. Thank you for respecting the hard work of this author.
This book is a work of fiction. Names, characters, places, and incidents either are products of the author's imagination or are used fictitiously. Any resemblance to actual events or locales or persons, living or dead, is entirely coincidental.
The author acknowledges the trademarked status and trademark owners of various products referenced in the work of fiction, which have been used without permission. The publication/use of these trademarks is not authorized, associated with, or sponsored by the trademark owner.

how the mind breaks

A DARK ROMANCE

USA TODAY BESTSELLING AUTHOR

DANI RENÉ

acknowledgments
thank yous

This dark story came about back in 2017, and was signed with a small publisher, released under the title, The Shattered Girl. When I got the rights back, I knew it needed polishing, and I wanted Tia and Braxton's story to be released again. And here it is!

I have to say a special thank you to Michelle Myers, for her support for this story. It's definitely not your average read, and she offered up advice to make this book shine. Thank you, babe!

The Street Team, you ladies work your ass off to get my name out there, thank you. From the bottom of my little black heart, THANK YOU!

My Deviants!! This group is like my own personal form of therapy. Thank you!! There is never a dull moment, and that's what makes me thankful for your love and support. It's not easy working with the intense stress and deadlines, but you always seem to brighten my day!

To my fellow authors who are there with advice, support, and just a general pick me up. Thank you. It means more to me than you know. Thank you for sharing my work with your readers, and giving me a friendship that is second to none.

To the bloggers, you ladies read, read, read, support, post, review, and you do it with a smile. Thank you!! We wouldn't be here if it weren't for you, so keep what you're doing, we appreciate you! #AllBlogsMatter!

Lastly, to the readers, thank YOU! It's because of you I'm able to put out book after book. Giving you what you ask for, and hopefully making you excited about the next book. Thank you for your reviews, keeping them SPOILER FREE ;) But most of all, thank you for buying our books. For your support, love, and encouragement.

Mad love, D x

dear Reader

This story is unconventional. It will be confusing at times because it has two timelines running parallel, but I hope you give it a chance.

It's dark, it's light, yet it's filled with love. It's unconditional love, which I hope will show you there is someone who will want you in your happy times as well as your dark moments.

Not all love stories are fairy tales, and not all fairy tales only have hearts and flowers. Like this story. You'll find none of those; instead, you'll find raw emotion, you'll find fear and darkness, but you'll discover how the depth of emotion we all search for can overcome any adversary.

Thank you for taking the time to read it. I hope in my words you find the light in their journey.

Mad love, Dani xo

playlist
the music

I Wanna Be Adored - The Stone Roses
Heart Heart Head - Meg Myers
Closer - The Chainsmokers, Halsey
Faded - Alan Walker
Monster - Aaron Richards
My Hell - Aaron Richards
Desire - Meg Myers
Sorry - Halsey
Hurts Like Hell - Fleurie
Tear You Apart - She Wants Revenge
Dark in my Imagination - of Verona

Find the playlist on Spotify

blurb
about the book

USA Today Bestselling Author, Dani René, brings you a dark, psychological romance a twisted ending you'll never see coming!

A dark past. A devastating secret. Two broken people.

Tia is focused on revenge, but she knows everything isn't what it seems. With a painful past that continues to haunt her, she needs vengeance. As her sanity becomes more fragile, there's only one person who can heal her. But it's the one person she doesn't want to allow inside her shattered psyche.

Braxton has been trained to kill, fighting on the front line. On returning home, he finds another war ravaging his world. Tia stumbles into his life, unraveling parts of him he's kept hidden for so long.

As they venture through a dark, sordid path filled with vengeance and blood, they know there's no way out, but to complete their mission.

Will a broken mind mend a shattered heart?

*Please note, this was previously published under the title The Shattered Girl.

dedication

this is for you

For those who struggle daily. Keep going,
you're strong, you're able, and you're more
than capable.

prologue

Rolling over, I stretch, feeling each muscle tense, then ease. My hair is matted to my head, and I'm sweaty. The nightmares have been fierce, and I can't remember much about them, but the fact that my tank top is stuck to my torso tells me I've been stressed in sleep, and I've also been tossing and turning.

When I glance at the time, I realize I'm late.

I'm always fucking late.

Pushing off the bed, I notice the blood on the pillow, which I kept between my legs for comfort. The crimson has seeped into the material of my cotton pillowcase. If I spent a little longer in bed, it would be all over the sheets.

I remember the first time I woke up to the coppery fluid. It wasn't because of me finally becoming a woman. Not in the sense that most girls do. No, my story is much darker than that. Much more violent.

Moving hurts.

You did it again.

No.

Shaking my head, I drag my gaze to my legs. They're red, stained.

Always.

It's your fault.

No. No.

"Leave me alone!" Shouting never helps, so I rise, then pad over to my bathroom. They've given me a beautiful apartment to stay in while I'm here. It's decked in white tiles, carpets, and the walls are painted a sterile gray. Nothing seems out of place, but it's not home. It can never be home. Everything here is perfect.

It's a lie.

Fucking lie.

"Jesus Christ, leave me alone."

It's all you do. Liar, liar, pants on fire.

I grip the steel taps and twist them, watching as the steam fills the room. In an attempt to calm down, I inhale deeply. Even if I try to focus, I know it will be futile. Nothing can help after the nightmares. I wait for the feeling of being cocooned in warmth, curled in the blanket of heat before stripping my dirty clothes off. Once I step beneath the cascading hot water, I revel in the prickling on my skin.

He will find you.

No.

Every day is the same song and dance. She loves to taunt me. To remind me of what's wrong with me. Even though she's become somewhat of a constant in my life, some*one* who understands, I know it's not *normal*.

They said it would stop. They told me I'd be okay. But it's a lie. I'll never be cured. How can I be cured when I was born this way? I pull at my hair, tugging it from the roots.

The burn is the only thing that's real. The one and only thing.

No, it's not.

"Leave me alone!" My throat burns from screaming so loud. I've been telling her to leave me alone, but she doesn't. "Why?"

Why me?

"Yes."

There wasn't a time I didn't know her, hear her, feel her. I used to get lost inside my head all the time. My teachers told me it was normal. They said all kids have imaginary friends. So, I believed them. I didn't chase her away then, and she's never left. She makes me do it.

Don't blame me.

"Fuck you!"

Never.

I'll never be the same.

the present
Tia

"Can you tell me about it, Tia?" Her voice is calm, but it doesn't still the war inside me. It doesn't allow me any reprieve from the thoughts. It's safer in my head. In the place where she is. My best friend.

She's the only one who understands.

No one else has ever understood.

"Tia, get out of there. I can see you're working through your mind. Don't hide."

It's so easy for her. She tells me this every time I'm in this goddamn chair, but I'm not like her. I'm broken and nothing can cure me. I'm not *normal* like other girls. Special.

I'm not like anyone.

I'm different.

Unique. But I don't see it.

"I'm . . . I don't hide. I'm just thinking. I

don't know." Shaking my head, I rake my hands through my hair and sigh when she sits back, her pen poised, waiting. She notes my movements. My words. My actions.

"Tell me about him."

Glancing up, I look at her kind eyes. "He's beautiful." I smile when I think about him and the first time we met. It's an honest grin. "When I first saw him, I didn't speak to him. I couldn't because he was too alluring. His friend flirted with me, but he never did. He always looked like he hated me. And I didn't know why, like he was pushing me away, and all I wanted was for him to pull me closer." I sigh, "But now that he's here, that he's with me, it's different."

"Tia, tell me. Do you think about him and the future?" she questions carefully.

Shaking my head, I try to focus. I feel tired today, and all the questions are confusing me. "I do, there are times I wonder if it will ever happen—forever. It's just a long fucking way away," I tell her honestly because it's what I believe.

She winces at my cursing. She always does. I like cursing. It feels good.

"What about his friend? He is… not good?" Her questions are cautious because she knows I can be volatile. Sometimes, I can't control what happens, so I just focus on his eyes, which I have memorized. When he looks at me, it's like there's a fire burning in his gaze.

"No, I want Braxton. It's always been him. Even when he hated me. Don't men who hate you love you more?" The question, when I voice it, sounds stupid. Something about him that lured me in. Something that I knew couldn't fight.

There's an intoxicating pull when those caramel eyes pin me to the spot. It's as if there are magnets holding me in place. I can feel myself being pulled into his forcefield.

Magnetic.

"He's magnetic," I tell her the word.

She nods slowly and jots down her notes.

She likes notes.

Always writing.

Always scrutinizing.

"I like that you have someone to confide in, other than me, of course. Do you feel the darkness when he's there?"

No, no, no. He's perfect—his mouth, his face, and his eyes. Even his body.

"It's safe when he's there. She doesn't come to me. Memories don't plague me. I don't feel like I need to go away, like I have to go into that place in my mind."

She encourages with a hand gesture for me to continue.

"I want to climb into him. Does that make sense? The safe place in my head is like him. It's light."

"Mmm . . .," she murmurs and writes furiously. The ding of the clock tells me our time is up. "I want you to think about this session. I want you to make sure you take your medication. It's only a precaution, but it will help. I'll see you in two days."

She rises from her chair. Perfectly poised. Beautifully feminine. Nodding, I shrug on my jacket and head for the door.

"Two days," I whisper before exiting her office. A lot can happen in two days.

the past

When I lift my gaze from the empty glass in front of me, it immediately falls on her. It always does. There's a smile on her face that seems to light up the room. It's the one she always gives him when he walks in. Although he's my best friend, I know what he does behind her back. And as much as I'd love to be her knight in shining armor, I know it will hurt them both.

She needs to find out on her own. I haven't told her. Perhaps I should. Ryker has been an asshole since we arrived home from Afghanistan, and I don't know how to make him see that what he's doing to her is wrong.

I'm biding my time for the moment she walks in on him or finds him with one of the sluts he favors over her. I'll be there to watch her fall. And when she does, I'll be the one who catches her, because when he breaks her heart and makes her cry, I'll kiss those tears away. I bet they'll taste as sweet as I imagine.

Six months, I've sat back and waited. I've been here in the wings just watching her. Taking her in, inch by inch. I know every curve of her body, every spot to touch that makes her giggle and tremble. That makes her eyes shimmer with intense need.

Sitting back on the soft leather sofa, I watch them interact as they always do, sweet and loving, romantic even. She leans over the bar to press a kiss to his cheek before she pours him another beer. He grins, but I know it's a lie. I've known Ryker since we were kids, and I know what type of man he's grown up to be.

Me? I'm not any better. I love it as dark and filthy as it comes.

The only difference is, if I had the girl I have my eye on, I wouldn't fuck her around like he's doing. I may enjoy a chase, but once I catch my prey, my focus is solely on her.

She's perfect . . . for me.

My name is Braxton, and I'd like to fuck my best friend's girlfriend until she can't walk. To take her incredibly lithe body and throw it around like a rag doll. I want those plump lips wrapped around the base of my dick while she swallows every inch.

Why? Because it's the only thing I think of every single fucking day.

Pushing up from the seat, I saunter toward the bar and slam my empty glass on the shiny oak counter, interrupting their sweet exchange of fuck knows what. I don't know how he can whisper sweet nothings in her ear now, and later tonight—when he blows her off for someone else—be balls deep in another woman.

"I need a refill."

She glares at me with those electric-blue eyes before grabbing my glass and turning to fill it up with the golden draught.

"Do you have to be such a dick to her?" Ryk bites out in frustration.

"Yeah, man. I do."

When she brings the glass back, I cock my head to the side and offer her a salacious grin, only to be met with a scowl. A sexy one at that. One that makes my dick hard. "Thank you." I drop my tone, softening it to a rumble, and I don't miss the glimmer in the stare she pins me with.

Turning my back to them, I pull out my phone and hit dial on the number for the office.

I need to head in to get the info on our latest target. An asshole running a trafficking ring on the border to Mexico. He's going to get what's coming to him — a bullet from my gun deep inside his skull.

The familiar, deep voice of Grant greets me from the other side of the line.

"Sweet cheeks, you bringing me one of those brewskies?" *Cheeky fucker.*

"Fuck off. We'll be there in fifteen. Be ready." With that, I hang up and down the ice-cold beer in a few gulps before pulling on my leather jacket. "Let's go, Ryk, you can fuck her later." I chuckle when I hear him sigh as I make my way out the door. Glancing over my shoulder, through the flawless glass pane, I notice her watching me. Tipping my two fingers in a mock salute, I wink at her before heading toward the car.

Soon, Tatiana. I'll be riding your sweet ass real soon.

"What the fuck, B?" Ryker sounds pissed off, which only makes me smile.

Ignoring my partner, I slide into the driver's seat of my sleek silver Aston. It purrs to life, and the radio blares as he slips into the passenger seat.

"Brax, why are you always such an asshole

with her?" he questions again.

"You're getting your cock sucked and fucked by every woman from here to God knows where when we're on the job, and you want to talk about me being a dick to her?" My retort doesn't go unnoticed; he regards me with as much animosity as I figured he would.

"Do you want her?" he grits out through clenched teeth.

Scoffing at his question, I pull out onto the main road and head south. We've got a meeting at headquarters, and I'm not getting into this with him while I'm driving. I ignore him and turn the radio up, hoping the rock sounds of The Killers singing "Mr. Brightside" will drown him out and diminish this need I have for that woman.

She's fucking gorgeous.

Long, flowing brown hair with thin strands of gold shimmer through the darker locks. Her tanned skin is exquisite, like smooth malt, honeyed from what I'm guessing to be Puerto Rican or Spanish roots. Those ice-blue eyes that shoot daggers at me every time I walk into the bar. And those curves, Jesus Christ, those curves that could make a sane man lose his mind.

Shaking my head to clear the images of all

the filthy things I'd love to do to her, I take the road toward the industrial side of town. Our HQ is in a warehouse on the docks, desolate, where no one else can find us. We're an elite squad of ex-Marines who feel that something needs to be done with the depraved, violent things happening in our city, and our country.

After being injured, I'd been sent home, and now I call the city of San Antonio home. The underground we patrol is not for the fainthearted. I'd seen shit when I was in other countries where killing and maiming was normal, but when I learned of what was going on in my own hometown, something had to be done. Ryker joined me not long after, and for three years, I've called Retribution—our squad—home.

As soon as I pull into the parking lot, my best friend is out of the car. Taunting him has become one of my favorite pastimes, and I watch him for a moment as he heads inside. I know he's angry because he knows I want her.

The only question is—*what's he going to do about it?*

Shoving the car door open, I follow him into the warehouse, nodding at Grant as I pass him. He's been with us for a couple of years, and he mans the phones and all the incoming inquiries.

"What's up, man? What crawled up Ryk's ass?" he growls. The man could easily pass for a basketball player at his height of seven feet. Built like a warrior from years gone by, he is one of the only men in here who could take me down with one fucking hand.

"He's an asshole," I bite back.

"Did you fuck his girl yet?" He chuckles, and I can't help but pin him with a glare.

We normally head to the bar where Tatiana works after a session at the gym, and I guess my eye fucking hasn't gone unnoticed.

"Not yet." Lowering my voice, I place my palms on his desk as I respond, "But when she catches him with his dick out, that's when I'll swoop in to pick up the pieces and make sure that tight little pussy is purring happily."

He guffaws as I turn to walk away. The place is deadly quiet tonight, but upon reaching the upper level, I find all the guys watching the large screen bolted to the wall.

The images that greet me are familiar because I recognize the nightclub that I've spent too much time in. Girls on every floor cater to you, especially in the VIP section where they're happy to drop to their knees for a wad of cash.

"What are we watching?" I question, flopping

onto the sofa beside Jake, one of the younger recruits.

"This is our next hit. Guy who owns the place is a high-stakes dealer." He drags his gaze from the screen and meets mine. "In girls, ammo, and drugs. Anything you want, he can get it. Any price, any age, any high."

My blood pressure skyrockets when the man I've been waiting for most of my adult live saunters onto the screen. He's old, wrinkled, with a potbelly to boot. He has two girls on either arm, girls who don't look like they're old enough to drink, let alone be hanging on an asshole old enough to be their grandfather. The idea makes bile rise into my throat.

I can't stop the anger that fuels me. "Let's take the fucker down."

My grunt is met with a loud, *"Yeah!"*

"We will. I want you and Ryk on the inside." Corp strides up to us, dressed in his combat uniform. He looks ever the general. A graying fifty-year-old ex-vet who's fitter than most twenty-year-olds, he's been through it all, lost men in battle, and now he's here, coaching us and training us to take down fuckers like the one we're about to nail.

"Sounds good, boss. Do you want to give

me the breakdown now?" I question, needing to get my hands dirty. Deep down, I thought I'd come back home, find a nice girl, and start a family. That didn't happen. I came home to my own nightmare. Now, revenge is all I need. And if it means killing every sonofabitch out there, I'll do it.

Corp shakes his head, glancing between my partner and me. "Tomorrow at ten, and don't be late." His warning is clear. Ryker's been playing at his tardiness for months now, and I'm sure Corp's going to send him packing if he doesn't take his job seriously.

Lifting my hand in a salute, I offer him my signature smirk.

Once he's disappeared into his office, the guys start yapping at the screen, which has me dragging my attention back to the images in front of me. There, in the throng of beautiful bodies, is a dark-haired vixen with the tiniest fucking skirt on. Her top is tight, hugging a pair of tits I'd love to slide my dick between. *Jesus, Tatiana.* She may as well be naked.

"Let's go." Pushing up, I grip Ryker's arm and tug him along behind me. It's time to pay a visit to the club and keep an eye on my new pet project.

the present

braxton

I saw her again today. It's the same every time. Her beautiful eyes pierce me. They fill me with need. An ache I haven't known in years. I've been broken for so long that I just don't understand the emotions racing through me. All I want to do is throw her over my shoulder and claim her. She's mine.

I'll make sure of it.

It's silent this evening. There isn't always this peace in this place, but tonight they've granted me a reprieve. The fear that runs through my veins doesn't heat, and I shiver. Lying back, I stare at the white ceiling. It's plain, nothing adorning it, no pattern to concentrate on. Although the small lightbulb that hangs from the center of the ceiling swings slowly as if a gentle breeze has just tickled it.

"Braxton." A soft murmur jolts my mind from racing through the darkness I get so lost in, and I sit up in bed. My door is closed, but I hear her.

Pushing up, I pad over to the exit. Pulling on the handle, I open it to find her standing in a white nightdress. Her long, flowing hair hangs loosely down to the middle of her back. Even with her hidden in darkness, she's still so luminous.

"Hey," I greet her with a smirk.

"Can you come out to play?" Her lips pout, her head tipping to the side as she regards me with those blue eyes that are alight with mischief.

I nod. Taking one last glance at the room, I step over the threshold and follow her down the hallway. It's deserted, just the way I like it. We've learned how to slip through the doors without being detected.

Long ago, we stumbled across this room with the swimming pool. It's massive, with glass ceilings which allow us to see the stars. She always tells me she loves my cock inside her when she's looking at the stars.

At the edge of the dark water, I tug off my tee and shove my slacks off. I'm not wearing anything underneath, and my thick cock hangs obscenely between my thighs.

"You're hard already?" She giggles.

"I'm always hard for you," I quip with a grin I know she likes. Without waiting, I dive into the cool water, and as soon as I surface, I see her watching me. Her form nude to my gaze. Long, slender legs poised to jump in to join me. Perky breasts taunt me with dark nipples.

As soon as the splash comes from beside me, I turn to her, and she wades toward me, wrapping her lithe legs around me. We fit. As if the gods above created us for each other.

"Fuck me, please. Make the pain go away," she begs, and I reach between us to find her slick entrance. My fingers taunt her while my mouth suckles her hardened nipple. My teeth graze along the flesh, eliciting a cry from her. A mewl that's so intoxicating it's as if I shot up with something strong and addictive.

"Did you play with yourself before you came to my room?" I question. My voice is low, demanding, and she will respond.

Tia nods, biting her lip in the most seductive way. Everything she does is to taunt me, but I wouldn't have it any other way, because this is how we were made to be. In our brokenness, we've found solace.

"Do you want it hard and deep?" Tipping my head to the side, I watch her eyes darken, and she nods again, her pearly whites sinking into that plump, lower lip.

Without warning, I drive into her. Rolling my hips, I seat myself inside her fully, savoring the tightness of her pussy. She always feels so good. I grip the globes of her ass as I bounce her on my dick. Her beautiful breasts tease me, and I latch onto a nipple, biting down hard, eliciting an erotic cry from her.

Her hands tangle in my hair, tugging me closer. I devour her body. She mewls when I thrust in harder, the water rocking us back and forth in our frenzy. Her body is tight around my cock, sucking me in deeper. Her slickness is making it difficult to hold back my release.

I pull out suddenly, and she snaps her burning gaze to regard me. "What—?"

"Kneel on the stairs," I order in a deep growl. She walks through the water and steps onto the lowest stair, kneeling. She glances back to find me behind her. My cock aligns with her wet entrance, and I grip her hips before driving in deep. Plunging into the most incredible cunt I've ever felt.

Fisting her long brown hair, I tug her head

back and watch as her spine arches beautifully. "That's it, baby, take me," I grunt as I fuck her violently.

This is what we're like.

Brutal. Ferocious. Rabid.

Her body pulses, and she cries out my name repeatedly, which sets me off, and I blast jet after jet of hot release inside her. Marking her. She's mine. Forever.

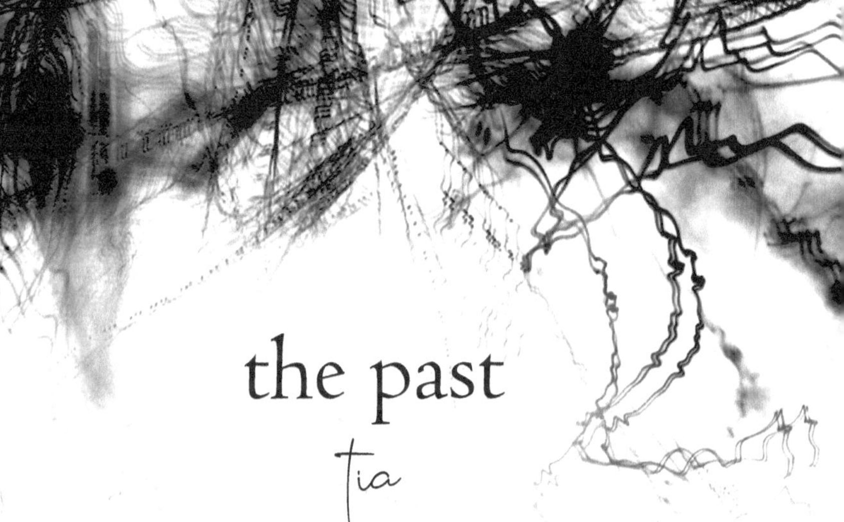

the past
Tia

Jesus, he's such a dick. My mind is in overdrive as I shut down the bar. The moment I laid eyes on him, I knew he'd be trouble, and since then, I've not been disappointed. *Braxton Carter is an asshole.* A fucking hot asshole, but one, nonetheless. It doesn't matter that every time I'm near him, I want to rip him to shreds. Literally.

Under that tough exterior, though, I know there's a monster craving to be unleashed. Those tight black tees he wears that mold to every sculpted inch of him have me salivating every time he walks in here and gives me that rude, crass personality.

But there are layers to that man.

I see them.

He's easy to read, someone who, under all

the macho shit, has a heart and he wears it on his sleeve. Although he does hide it around me, under the overconfident persona, I noticed how he'd watch me. There's a darkness in his gaze that calls to mine. It drags me in and magnetizes me. And with every stare, and each wolfish grin, I find myself wanting him. I've wanted him for months.

There's something animalistic about him that makes my body quiver. When I chose Ryker, I knew I wouldn't fall for him. It was easier than messing around with emotions when all I need is revenge.

Even though it's all part of the plan, somehow, I know I've fucked up, because deep down, I have a feeling something is about to break, and all my secrets will come pouring out. Call it women's intuition, or whatever the fuck you want to, but I know they're hiding something, and I'll find out what it is.

Strolling over to my shiny Lexus, I slide into the driver's seat and moan at the feel of the leather against my skin. My work uniform doesn't leave much to the imagination. The tiny pair of shorts and halter-neck top shows more skin than I'd normally expose, but when I'm at the bar, I've got to play the part.

Starting the engine, I connect my iPhone to the dock and hit dial on the number I need. "Pussycat." *Fucking dickhead.*

"I told you not to fucking call me that. Is it so difficult for your tiny brain to understand?" The chuckle I'm met with annoys me further. "Where's Laney?"

"Hold on, don't get the panties you don't wear in a twist," he growls down the receiver. I hear muffled voices and then I hear her.

"Hey, sweet cheeks, what's up? You going out tonight?" Elaine is one of those girls that can party until four in the morning and still look like she's had eight hours of sleep the next day. We've worked together for months, and she's the only reason I've gotten closer to the man I've trained myself to kill.

"Let's hit the club. I have a feeling we'll find what we're looking for tonight."

She laughs before responding quietly, "Did you see him?" She asks me the same thing every night I call. And every night, I tell her the same thing.

"You know I did. The problem is, I can't let myself feel anything for someone I'm just going to walk away from." Turning right, I drive down the road toward my apartment building. It's not far to the penthouse I've called home for the past six months, and with the streets being so quiet this time of evening, I'm pulling into my parking spot in record time. I turn off the engine and sit back, waiting for my best friend to tell me what she does every day.

"There's no need for love, Tia, you know this. Just fuck him, get him out of your system, and move on." Laney's voice is a whisper, and I know she doesn't want her asshole boyfriend to hear her. I glance at the phone. Even though she can't see me, I feel as if her gaze is trained on me.

Shrugging, I grab the device and hold it against my ear. "He's hot, but he couldn't handle my crazy ass." I glance around, noticing the security guard is in the small office which sits inside the garage close to my parking spot. "Listen, I'll see you in ten. I'll catch a cab so we can have those shots you keep telling me about."

"Yes!" she shrieks loudly. "Bye, sweet cheeks. I'll be waiting."

Exiting the car, I shut the door and push the button, locking it with a small beep.

"Ms. Tatiana," a deep baritone voice greets me, and I nod at the guard who seems to always work the nightshift, and I wonder briefly if he has a family waiting on him. He's about six feet tall and built like a fucking steel door. I doubt anything can get past that. Once I step into the elevator, I push the button for the top floor. My beautiful penthouse. The only good thing I got when I decided to exact my revenge.

Life hasn't been easy on me, but when Mr. Henlow found me, took me in, and trained me to kill, I knew there was one person who would one day feel my wrath. Henlow runs an undercover organization that "cleans up messes," as he puts it. When I told him about why I wanted to join him, he not only offered me free reign of the gym, trainers, and weapons, he gave me what I needed most—a promise to kill the man who hurt me.

I close my eyes and attempt to focus on the here and now. My mind flits back to Brax earlier tonight, and I instantly feel a buzz as if I'd taken a shot of pure alcohol. The man is sinful.

With messy brown hair and those caramel eyes, they do me in every time. He's got lips most women would kill for, bow-shaped and full—pink and delicious. I'd love to bite them, suck on them until he's growling his need. Since the first time I saw him, I wanted to meet the beast he hides, the monster that's only shown himself a handful of times.

His chiseled jaw with a light dusting of stubble is enough to have me squirming. His toned muscles are clear in those shirts he favors, and I know he's strong enough to lift me, push me against the wall, and fuck me hard.

Simply put, he's made for fucking.

Long nights of imagining my fingers digging into the smooth skin of his shoulders, scratching my nails down his back as he rams into me, have haunted me. Shaking my head, I watch the numbers light up. As the elevator reaches the thirtieth floor, the doors slide open, and I step into my foyer.

I'm the only one with access to this floor, which gives me my own private hallway leading up to the front door. Once inside, I turn on the overhead lights to the lowest setting and turn on the sound system. Something loud and fucked-up is needed. *Cradle of Filth.* Heavy metal booms through the surrounding speakers, and I tug off my Doc Martens and pad into the kitchen.

Grabbing a bottle of ice-cold beer from the fridge, I head into the bedroom and step into my walk-in closet. Black, red, black, purple. Pulling out the shortest jet-black denim skirt I own and a small purple tank top that's possibly too tight, I head back into the room and shed my clothes. I told Laney ten minutes, but I need a shower.

Taking a long gulp of beer, I set the bottle down and stroll into my *en suite*, turning on the shower, and before the water is even hot, I step under the spray. The icy needles hit me like a slap to the face, and I savor the chill that seeps through my veins. After seeing Braxton, I need this.

Some may think I'm a bitch for lusting after my boyfriend's best friend, but I'll never cheat; that's not in my nature. The thing about it is, I know what Ryker's doing, and I'm using him as much as he's using me. What I need from him is a confession, which I'll never get, so I need to catch him in the act.

This is a business transaction between us, even though Ryker has no clue. He thinks I'm the clueless girlfriend, when I'm the one who can kill him in the blink of an eye.

I came to San Antonio with one thing in mind. When Henlow told me the man I'm looking for is here, I left New York the next day. It's only been six months, and I've gotten his schedule down to a T.

Using Ryker to get the information I need is easy because I don't love him. So I figure, why not enjoy it while I can? Have two hot men wanting to keep me safe. It's sweet really, if only they knew I'm the one they should be scared of.

Grabbing my body wash, I lather up and feel my muscles relax from the warm water and the scent of sandalwood and lavender. Closing my eyes, I picture him, Ryker, stroking my back and shoulders. His strong hands tease the muscles in my neck, pressing the knots until they're all gone. His soft lips taste my bare skin, and I can't help moaning.

Another pair of hands trail down my arms, and I find caramel pools dark with lust piercing me. *"You're needy for me, aren't you?"* The rough tone in his voice sends a shiver down my spine.

"She wants us both," the voice behind me says, but he's wrong. I don't want them both. Ryker's hand grips my throat, and in my mind's eye, I watch as Braxton bares his teeth. The animal is fighting for what's his—me.

My hands dip between my thighs, stroking and teasing my slick core as I imagine them both touching me. Strong hands, corded muscles tense and release. Two of them, one of me, shivering under the ministrations of these talented men.

"I know you crave my dick, Tatiana," the hiss of Brax's voice taunts me in my fantasy, and my fingers fly over my clit. *"Don't you?"* His teeth

graze my earlobe, biting down, causing me to cry out. *"Come for me, Vixen. Make that tight cunt soak your fingers."* His filthy words send me over the edge, and I shout out his name like a prayer.

I snap my eyes open and find myself alone in the shower, trembling from an intense orgasm. The shower turns cold, and a shiver wracks through me, chasing its way down my spine.

I'm a fucking mess.

The thought hits me as I step out onto the fluffy mat and grab a towel. Wrapping myself in the soft material before glancing at my reflection in the large mirror, I find an unrecognizable woman staring back at me.

You're the mess. You're all fucked up. No one can save you.

She taunts me. She tells me what I don't want to hear. If only I could rid myself of her, but I know I can't. She's right. No one can save me. Grabbing for the bottle on the countertop, I flick the lid open and shake my medication into my palm. Swallowing the three pills I've had to take from an early age, I inhale slow and deep, exhaling the thoughts that haunt me.

It doesn't take long for me to calm down and head to the bedroom to get dressed.

It's never going to end.

Stepping into Innuendo, I feel every pair of eyes follow me. Girls. Guys. Everyone.

"You're like the siren in here tonight," Laney whispers beside me.

"I'm not looking for it. I just want a drink." As soon as I head to the bar, the tall blonde barmaid strolls up to me, popping her pink bubblegum, and immediately, my skin prickles.

Slut.

Shut up.

"Beer, bottle's fine."

She nods without greeting, turns to the fridge behind her, and slams a cold bottle onto the counter. I dump the five dollars on the dirty wood and grab my drink.

"Thanks." I don't know why I say anything since she can't hear me. The music vibrates through the walls, into my body, and my chest thuds with the melodic rhythm.

Laney orders her pink girly drink, and I turn to regard the talent. Not one man catches my eye. I know why. None of these men are Braxton. If only I wasn't here on a job, I'd be able to do something about the attraction to him.

My best friend grins, and when I drag my

gaze over to her, my heart catapults out of my chest and into my throat.

"Hello, Vixen." Pools of caramel melt into me, sending a warm tingle down my spine, hitting low in my back. I recognize the feeling from earlier when I was alone in the shower. When all I wanted was those hands on me. He offers a grin, which sets my nerves alight.

"What are you doing here?" I ask, attempting to sound cool and calm, but I'm not sure I can be around Braxton. Glaring at him, I wait for a response, which he gifts as a grin that shows off his dimples.

A glimmer of mischief dances in his eyes, as if he's been dying to break me, and the way he's looking at me with that overconfident, narrowed gaze sends another sizzle of warmth through me.

"I'm always here." He glances around, but only for a second, as if nobody else is worthy of those beautiful, honeyed orbs but me. "Question is, what are you doing here dressed like that?" The sneer he offers angers me, but the way his stare trails from my fuck-me heels, up my bare legs, to my skimpy top—stopping momentarily on my tits—finally settling on my own gaze, sends a thrill of anticipation over my skin, heating me and turning me molten. I could easily erupt from the mere look.

"I'm here to have some fun." Lifting my bottle, I press it to my lips and slowly gulp down the alcohol I didn't realize I needed until Braxton's heated gaze settled on me. Jesus, this man is going to fuck me up.

You're going to hurt him. You always do.

"Come on, Vixen, dressed like that? That's not fun; that's looking for trouble."

Laney stares between us, flicking her gaze back and forth.

"I'm going to the ladies' room," she mumbles, and before I can respond, she spins on her heel and leaves me with Braxton. *Fuck.*

"Tell me, Vixen," he persists. Stalking closer to me, he steps into my personal space. As much as I want to shove him out of it, I bask in his warmth. "Do you like men seeing you dressed like a common slut?" His words are venom laced with jealousy. He's trying to hurt me, but what he doesn't know is, I'm shut off from slurs. I've heard worse shit growing up. My father was evil, and he loved to throw his weight around. Now, when I hear the word *slut,* I can't help but smile, because it does shit to me.

Braxton's hand grips my hip. It's the first

time he's actually touched me, and it feels more intimate than any of the times I've had Ryker's hands on me. The searing heat of his fingertips scorches me through the thin material, and I'm sure he's going to set me ablaze soon.

"I do," I finally answer him. "Since my boyfriend fucks around, why can't I?" I bite back.

The shock on his face is evidence that he knew. I wouldn't be surprised if they ended up sharing the women that I know Ryker's fucking behind my back. But then again, when I look at Braxton, he doesn't seem to be interested in any of the females in this club.

"What? You were too scared to tell me?" I choke out a laugh and push myself against him, so my breasts flatten against his rock-hard body. "I'm not a fragile little girl, Brax. I can handle bad news," I hiss in his ear.

His body trembles under my palm, which I smooth on his chest. With my drink in hand, I leave him gaping at me, and stalk toward the toilets to find Laney, but what I find is not the girl I was expecting. Instead, a sight that sets the wheels in motion for my next fix.

"Oh God, yes, yes, deeper," the blonde bartender moans loudly as she gets slammed against the wall. Her long legs are wrapped around the taut waist of the man sliding into her, driving and plunging so fast and so fucking deep I can feel it.

"Fuck yes, take it, bitch," the voice growls as he shudders, violently coming inside her.

"Hey, baby, I didn't know you were here." My voice is syrupy sweet, so sweet, in fact, that I have a toothache. The blinding rage I feel when I look at the woman my boyfriend was just plowing into is all I need.

The fuel to turn my body into a weapon.

The venom drips into every nerve in my body.

The poison that seeps into my blood pumping through me.

It's then that I see red.

the present

Tia

It's quiet in here today. In my mind and in the room. She watches me like she always does with caring scrutiny. I know what's coming. Since I mentioned Brax the last time I was here, she's been curious. I don't want to talk about him, but it's inevitable.

When I think of him, my heart races, my body aches, and my mind is filled with images of what I'm like when I'm with him.

A normal life.

But I'll never be normal. I need to accept my fate. Just like my mother did.

"Does Braxton know what you did or didn't do?" she questions softly. Shaking my head swiftly, I regard her, but before I can respond, she questions, "Care to tell me what actually took place when you saw them?" Her head tips to the side, curiosity marring her pretty features.

"No, he doesn't know." I fidget with my skirt. "I . . . It hurt. My body ached all over. It was a strange feeling, like electricity shooting through every part of me. And then the black . . . There was red also, bright, dark, luminous, and then I was lost. It was . . . I mean momentarily. It was only for a few moments, but..." Shuddering, the memory is still fresh in my mind. How Braxton saved me from myself. He was there, playing hero while I was losing my shit. I was broken, my mind was broken. I knew it. I've always known it. And Braxton seeing me like that didn't make a difference.

Fuck, I didn't care what Ryker thought of me. It was his best friend I wanted to impress. Braxton was the one I didn't want to find out just how fucked up I truly was. I didn't want him to know the woman inside was broken.

Shattered.

Just a mental, fucked-up basket case.

Somehow, in six months, Braxton was the one who'd woven himself so deep in my heart and mind that all I could think about was him. It was as if he was in my bones. In the marrow, just a part of me I couldn't erase.

"Did you hurt her, Tia?" she asks, dragging

me from my spiral into the darkness.

Shaking my head, I shut my eyes. Truth is, I don't know. I can't remember. Ryker told me I was crazy; perhaps he's right. Maybe I did do all those things so many times. All those bad things. All the lives that have been taken, maybe it was me. But then again, Braxton was there. He didn't say bad things to me. He didn't tell me I'm broken.

That's what Dad used to tell me.

"Tia, do you always go there when things are tough?" Her eyes bore into me. It pains me. I hate when people look at me, when they really stare at me. It's as if they can see the darkness swirling inside me.

"Yes, it's easier." Dragging my gaze away from her, I allow it to flit over the room. All the things—chairs, books, potted plants, windows, and the fish tank—I take into account every part of the office.

I can feel the curiosity in her posture. As if she's drenched herself in it like she has her perfume. She furrows her brows before asking, "What makes it easy?"

"I'm not crazy when I'm there. People don't disregard me or my actions because of who I am. Or what I've done. Nobody can hurt me there."

My voice sounds far away. It's as if I'm having an out-of-body experience. Sometimes this happens, and I feel unstable. I feel out of control. Like I'm floating on a cloud, and nobody can touch me; but then, that's not good because I'm not here, grounded, and that's when my mind plays tricks on me. Nobody understands. They don't get why I'm like this, so I just allow myself to flow into nothing.

"You're not crazy, Tia. You've been through so much. You've seen things that have scarred your mind. It's perfectly natural to break the way you did," she confirms in a motherly tone. "Your mind has given you a reprieve. It's the way you've found to cope. It's normal, Tia."

I glance at her then, really take her in. There's no smile on her lips. She's not lying.

Am I normal?

No, you're not.

"I can't . . . this . . . I mean . . ." Pushing off the sofa, I grab the coat I was wearing when I walked into her office, needing to get out of here.

"Tia, look at me." She rises, following me to the door. "You'll never heal if you walk away every time it hurts." She's right, but there's nothing I can do. I can't look at the dark parts of me. I self-destruct when I do that.

"I'm destructible. Memories, my past, everything makes me fragile. It's how my mind breaks when I go back there."

She shakes her head, but I have to look away. The way she's staring at me makes me feel almost normal. She insists, "No, it makes you strong. You know why?"

I turn to regard her, wondering where she's going with this, so I shake my head, hoping she'll offer some form of explanation as to why the darkness takes hold of me so often.

"Because you're fighting to survive. Because you *have* survived. Go to him. Go to Braxton and talk to him."

Nodding, I offer a smile. "Thank you, I need to go."

"I hope I see you soon, Tia. This will help. You just need to open yourself up to it."

the past

braxton

As soon as her sweet little ass sashayed away from me, it took all my restraint not to go after her. But I'm a man, I followed, and that's when she was met with the image of her boyfriend nailing someone else at the back of the club.

Things happened so quickly, all I needed was to make sure she was safe. So, I did. I knew she'd lose it when her body went rigid. The moment I pulled her off the blonde bimbo Ryker was fucking, she slumped in my arms.

Her friend pulled her into the ladies' restroom, leaving me staring at the closed door while Ryker tried to clean up the bloody mess of the barmaid that spread her legs for him. Slipping onto the barstool, I order a beer and take another look around, sweeping the floor area for cameras. The place is packed, but I pick out the security like they're fucking glow sticks in the dark. Ten in total. Easy pickings.

"I'm leaving." My best friend's voice comes from behind me.

I spin on my stool to find Ryker staring at me with rage blooming in his eyes. His face is red, angry, and I wonder why he even feels anything since it's his doing. This is what he wanted.

"What? We just got here." Offering him a grin, I know I'm pissing him off even more. Tia needed to release the anger of him cheating, so I don't blame her for beating up the chick.

He shrugs on his jacket and gives me a smirk. "You can have her." With that, he pivots and leaves me frowning at his disappearing form. Shaking my head, I lift my bottle and take a long swig of alcohol.

"Is the cheating fucker gone?" The scent of her engulfs me, and I turn to find my little vixen sidling up to me. Her hand trembles as she strokes the lapel of my leather jacket.

"He's gone. What was that back there? Did you blackout or something?"

She falters at the question, which intrigues me further. "I don't like stress. It makes my blood pressure drop, and I faint. It's something I've had to deal with since I was a kid. Nothing's wrong with me." Something about her defensive attitude has alarm bells going off around me, but I ignore them and down my beer.

"Let's have a drink," I offer, signaling the bartender for another beer. She nods, and I lift two fingers. "Seeing him with the barmaid set you off?" I meet her sapphire orbs that look like they hold too many secrets.

"Yeah, I guess I just wanted confirmation he was cheating before I did anything stupid." Her words drip pain, and I'm more intrigued by this beauty than ever before.

"Anything stupid like beat someone up?" I arch a brow at her, but she ignores me.

When our drinks arrive, she grabs hers and downs almost half the cold beer. "Brax," she murmurs, her hand tracing circles on the bar. "Why do you hate me? I always thought you wanted to fuck me."

The innocence in her tone and the filthy words are a contradiction, but when I glance at her again, I notice there's no purity in her. She's far from innocent, and I'm already growing hard just thinking about the dirty things I want to do to those plump lips.

"I've wanted you since the moment I walked into the bar where you work. But you chose

Ryker." I shrug it off. "I'm always up for a good fuck, Vixen. That is . . . if you are." Winking, I finish my beer and rise to my feet. I offer her my hand, and when her fingers twine with mine, I tug her along with me. "Where's your friend?" I question, and we both turn at the same time to find the pretty girl being twirled around between two men.

"She's busy."

"Don't you want—?"

"She's fine," Tia bites back and stalks to the door, leaving me to follow in the wake of her beeline for the exit. I don't know if we will get to fucking because I don't want to use her, but as they say, a revenge fuck is better than wallowing in pity. Granted, that's not what *they* say; that's what I say.

In the cab, I sit beside her, fighting the urge to touch her. The ride back to her apartment is silent, and the tension between us is palpable — a living, breathing entity. I'm afraid it's about to strangle us both.

"Here we are." The taxi driver glances in the rearview mirror, and I hand him a hundred, waving him off when he offers change.

"Thanks," I mutter pushing open my door.

Tia is out of the car in a flash, and when I

exit, I find her at an entrance to an immaculate apartment building, which looks like it's meant to be out in the middle of New York City, housing CEOs and celebrities.

"You live here?" My brows crease in confusion. For a bartender, she must earn a shitload to live on one of the city's most expensive blocks.

"There's a lot you don't know about me, Mr. Carter," she quips playfully and steps inside. The security guard glances up and smiles, nodding in a friendly greeting, but he doesn't actually say anything. I realize in that instant I should have looked into the dark-haired vixen. I don't know anything about her, and for some reason, I feel uneasy about that. My instincts kick in, and when we step into a private elevator, I wonder if this is a good idea. I can certainly take her down if need be, but I'm always careful with the people in my life.

"Are you going to tell me how a medium-wage bartender lives in one of the most prominent pieces of real estate in the city?"

She shrugs before answering, "Daddy can afford it, so I take advantage." Her response is rehearsed, which further sets my bullshit radar on full alert.

"And I'm meant to believe that?" I turn to her, meeting those eyes that hold more secrets than I care to toy with.

"No, I didn't ask you to. You asked a question, and I gave the general response everyone expects." She shrugs me off when I step closer to her. Something about her makes me want to know more, but there's something else that makes me want to push her away.

"I don't have time for bullshit, Tia," I bite out. Anger burns through me like a forest fire, and I turn to her, pushing her against the wall. I press my body against hers and lean in, our mouths inches apart.

This is the closest I've ever been to her, and my God, she's incredible.

"Do. Not. Fucking. Lie. To. Me." My voice is ice as I enunciate each word so she doesn't think I'm playing around. I've been through too much to have some woman fuck up my focus. Especially one playing games.

I don't miss the full body shudder that wracks her at my growl. Smirking down, I watch her face morph into a sultry smile. She reaches out for my chest, placing a hand on my pec, but she doesn't push me away.

"This what you wanted, Vixen?" Reaching

one hand down, I maneuver myself under her skirt before slipping my fingers between her slim thighs and stroking the soft silk that cups her cunt.

"Yes," she responds with conviction.

"Good, because you're going to get fucked. You're going to soak my cock in that sweet honey I know you've been aching to give me, and then you're going to suck me clean. Do you understand me?"

Again, she nods with confidence that has me bulging in my jeans. *Perfect.*

Stepping away from her, I watch as the doors slide open, depositing us on the top floor, leading to the penthouse suite. She's hiding something, and I'll find out what it is.

Without a word from her sassy mouth, she opens the front door and allows me to enter an apartment that looks like it's ready for a photoshoot. There's nothing personal that stands out as we walk into the space.

The click of the lock behind me causes me to pivot. The tanned goddess stalks toward me like I'm her prey, but that's where she's wrong. I'm the hunter. Her gaze glowers, as if she's someone else for a moment, like there's another entity inside her, and I wonder if there is.

"Are you sure you're ready for this? I'm not the nice girl you may think I am." She trails a French-manicured nail down the zipper of my leather jacket. The movement is slow, erotic, and taunts me, slowly ebbing away at my restraint.

"Nice girl? Who told you I think that? When I look at you, I see a very bad girl." I grip her wrist, tugging her against me. Her body is small, pliable under my touch. She lifts her gaze up to mine, meeting my eyes with an indignant stare. "I've dreamt of you. Fantasized about having you on your fucking knees, sucking me off."

Without a smart remark, she drops to her knees as I brace myself against the kitchen counter. My fingers curl around the cool marble, gripping the edge with a white-knuckle hold. The goddess peeking up at me through her thick, dark lashes looks like a fucking porn star.

Her fingers tug at my belt buckle while I shrug out of my jacket, then I watch her make quick work of pulling down my jeans. As soon as her soft hand fists me, I let out a low groan. A smile spreads on her lips, and her tongue flicks out, licking at my arousal. Plump lips engulf the crown of my dick as she lowers her mouth on my length. It's slow, torturous, but I love every fucking minute of it.

She takes my entire shaft into her mouth, the tip hitting the back of her throat as she bobs her head back and forth, all the while maintaining eye contact with me. It's one of the most beautiful things I've ever seen. Those blue eyes peeking up at me cause my body to turn hot with desire. She has the face of innocence, but she swallows my dick like a pro.

I've been dreaming of this day for far too long. When she hums, the vibrations send me into overdrive. I reach for her, pulling her off my cock until she's standing flush with me. Her lips are swollen and begging for mine, which I graciously gift her.

Crashing my mouth on hers, my tongue darts out, tasting the sweetness that is Tia, a dark-haired stranger I know nothing about. I trail my hands down her arms, gripping her hips, pulling her against me. My body is on fire with need as I lower my hands to her ass, lifting her to wrap her legs around my waist.

"Bedroom," I growl against her lips, and she points behind her.

Following the hallway, I find the master bedroom, which is vast with a king-sized bed and cream-colored sheets. We tumble onto the mattress together, me hovering over her, nestled between lithe thighs that hold me steady. Heat engulfs me when she lifts her hips, and I feel the warmth of her core at my bare shaft.

"I'm going to fuck you so hard, Vixen," I vow. I'll make sure she remembers me, remembers this night forever. Kneeling between her thighs, I tug at her tiny top to find the most incredible set of tits I've ever seen. Her nipples are dark and pebbled, and I can't help salivating at the sight of them.

the past

Tia

He tastes like sin—every inch of him—but he also tastes like salvation. Like light. Calmness. I devour it, like a demon feeding off his soul, as I lick into his mouth. His tongue swirls with mine, and I become addicted. My veins burn, spark, lighting up with need.

Addiction comes in many forms, but this is pure. As if he's going to save me from the darkness that clouds my mind. His body is heavy over mine, pressing me into the mattress, while he murmurs dirty words, filthy promises, and I want them all.

He reaches for his jeans, pulling out a foil wrapper, which I know we don't need. I place a hand on his before he rips the condom open. "I'm safe…" I blurt out, then allow my words to filter off and I don't know how to tell him I've never actually had Ryker inside me. Never once had him filthy me up. "I…"

"Talk to me," Brax murmurs, urging me for the truth I find so difficult to utter.

"I'm safe, I've not been with anyone in a while, not even Ryk." When I look at him, understanding burns in his eyes. "Just take me."

He nods but doesn't respond. Instead, he drops it on the floor. I've never asked for it, never wanted to beg a man to fuck me, but when those caramel pools regard me, I know what I want.

My mind is awash with nothing but him. For the first time in a long while, all I see is the man before me, not images that haunt me. His body—chiseled, taut, and warm—hovers over me for a long moment, as if he's waiting for something. For me.

All my life, men have used me. In more ways than I care to talk about, or think about, for that matter. When I take someone home, I'm the one in control, because men hurt and maim. But this man is something else entirely.

He doesn't fuck me yet; instead, he teases me. Rolling his hips, he teases my entrance while his mouth devours my breasts and nipples. They're peaked and painfully hard. His tongue taunts them, and his teeth bare down on them, biting to give me just enough pain that shoots to my core.

Gently, he moves higher, planting hot kisses on my neck, up to my earlobe, where he tugs the flesh between his teeth. The low growl that emanates from him vibrates through my chest and deep within my core.

In turn, my body is alight with need and desire. My fingers grip his shoulders, and my nails dig into the skin, as if I'm about to draw blood. I've never felt a craving like this before. Such a fierce need to have someone, to feel someone.

When he finally puts me out of my misery and slowly slides into me, connecting us, I cry out. My body is open for him, accepting him inside my madness, and I crave everything he's giving. He plunges into me, driving deep into my core. I feel everything below my belly button tighten, causing a whimper to fall from my lips.

His mouth once again lowers to my hardened nipples, biting down on them, sending shockwaves of desire coursing through me. He's a drug. It feels as if I've shot him into my bloodstream. My head falls back as my eyes flutter closed. The images and memories choke me in their grasp, causing me to spiral, down,

down, down. No, please, no. "Tia!"

A deep rumble breaks through my darkness, and I glance up to find caramel eyes staring down with concern. Our bodies are still connected. He's inside me. "I—"

"Look into my eyes," he orders quietly. I obey, watching his orbs swirl with honey and gold. "Feel me," he commands again, and I do. Every inch of him slides into me, hitting a spot inside of me that has my toes curling into the sheets.

My hands on his shoulders grip him as if he's my lifeline. As if he's going to save me. "Brax!" His name falls from my lips. It's not a moan or a cry of ecstasy; it's something else altogether. My body clings to his.

"That's it. Feel me. That's me fucking you. My dick owning your pussy." With every word, he slides in deeper than the time before. I'm not sure how it's possible, but he does. "Come for me. Give me your pleasure. I want every drop."

My body convulses at his words, and my nails dig into his shoulders. Ripping skin. Tearing at him. It's then that I see it.

Red. Copper. Claret.

The lifeforce of him seeping from his smooth, creamy skin. I revel in it.

I want to bathe in it.

He grunts, thrusting deeper, and I feel his warmth filling me. He stills for a moment, and I lick at the fluid on his shoulder, tasting the sharp metal flavor on my tongue. When he slips out of me and I glance down to look at his body, I really take him in—chiseled, toned, beautiful.

He has scars, but I don't ask about them. Small, silver markings all over his torso. There's a prominent V that dips toward his now softening cock, and thick, muscled thighs look strong enough to hold me up while he fucks me against any wall.

"Come here." He reaches for me with a smile. Circling me in his arms, I place my head on his chest, listening to his heart pump life into him, through him. The beat in my own heart calms my erratic breathing and seems to match his, to want that same rhythm.

I've had sex before, I've fucked, but this felt . . . real. Different.

"What's going on in that pretty little head?" His fingers reach for my chin, lifting my face until my eyes meet his. I knew he'd fuck me up because when I look into those shimmering orbs, I see it. He doesn't want to say it, or act like it, but I see it.

Emotion.

Not love. But concern, affection.

"Nothing. Why?" He doesn't answer me, instead shakes his head and lies back, tugging me into his side where I fit easily. I mold to the grooves and dents as if I was a part of him once, and now I'm back where I started.

The thought scares me. But as fear lingers in the back of my mind, I have it to myself.

She's not here. And as my eyes flutter closed, she doesn't come.

I have peace.

***

Rousing from a dreamless sleep, I roll over and find the sheets cold, my bed empty.

You're stained now. He's marked you.

No. No. No.

Did you think he wanted you? That he'd fuck you and fall in love?

I swing my legs over the edge of the bed. Rising to my feet, I pad into the bathroom and freshen up. My reflection doesn't taunt me, and I notice a soft pink in my cheeks.

Stained. Tainted.

One night with him, and I was free.

"I didn't know how long you'd sleep."

A deep, raspy voice startles me, and I yelp in surprise. Pivoting, I find Brax at the threshold of the room watching me, wearing only a pair of jeans. He's barefoot and shirtless with his arms crossed in front of him.

"What—?"

"You think I'd leave after last night?" He tips his head to the side, regarding me with those captivating golden pools I seem to get lost in too quickly.

"No. I mean, yes. You weren't in bed," I state matter-of-factly.

"I wasn't because I was making you breakfast." My gaze snaps to his in shock. "I do know how to cook, so I figured you wouldn't mind waking up to something to eat, and perhaps coffee?" His lips quirk as his eyes narrow, his shoulder resting on the doorjamb.

"I suppose, yes." Dropping my gaze, I focus on the tiles, counting them one by one. Slow. Focus. Breathe.

"Hey." His hands reach for me. They're warm, and he smells like food, like sustenance, and I realize that this man may be the end of my pain.

Maybe he's my peace.

My salvation.

No, I can't focus on someone else.

I need me, only me.

I'll hurt him. I always hurt them. She'll make me; she'll tell me I must. There's no one else who can get me out of this. I've been alone for too long to falter now. I've been tasked to do a job, so that's what I'll do.

"Vixen, look at me," he implores me quietly with a gentle touch. When I drag my gaze up to his, I find warmth. So fucking addictive, I'm already losing all restraint. "Where do you go? What's inside here?" He taps my temple lightly. Just the touch alone sends a shiver of delight through me.

"I protect others." My response falls from my lips before I can think, earning me a frown from him. The look of confusion on his handsome face instills fear in my heart because I can't tell him why. His gaze is transfixed on me. "I can't talk about it. Can we eat?" I change the subject, hoping he doesn't press further. Thankfully, he doesn't. Instead, he pushes his body against mine, which has heat surging down my spine, over my skin, into every nerve in my body.

"I'd love to. How about I get a little more acquainted with that beautiful pussy?" The side of his mouth lifts in that sexy side grin that has a flurry of butterflies wakening in my belly.

"What makes you think last night was anything other than a one-time thing?" I quip.

He leans in, whispering in my ear, "The fact that you're standing here all wet and needy for me to make you come again. Also, you've not yet asked me to leave, which means you're aching again. Something about me makes you want it. *I* make you want it."

His words reveal everything that's running through my mind because I do. I want it; I want him.

But I can't. I should push him away, tell him to leave. He shouldn't be here.

And when he steps back, I have every intention of telling him so, but you know what? I don't. Why? Because I'm a fucking masochist. I want to feel, and even though I know there'll be death, I don't let him go. Instead, I let him eat my pussy until I can't walk.

the present

Tia

"Close your eyes, Tia." I do. "Relax and breathe." My lungs fill with much-needed air. As if I'm floating. Her stillness calms me, giving me a reprieve from the storm raging in my mind.

I'm on a cloud, and she's an angel watching over me.

So quiet, so serene, giving me what only he gives me. Peace.

My eyes flutter as memories start appearing, and as much as I want to open my eyes to clear them, I don't. I allow myself to feel, to drift into the hypnotic dream she's telling me to find. My mind drifts back, back, back . . . to that day . . . It's cold, so cold. My head hurts. It's a violent pounding in my brain, as if it's about to shatter my skull. "I want you to remember the day it happened. When your life changed for the first time." I nod. I must have because she is quiet for a while.

"Momma, what are you doing?" She's there; I see her. She's coming toward me. Her dark curls are pinched tight. Her chocolate skin glistens with sweat as if she's exerted herself. I don't remember why. Or where she's been. She looks different, no longer the smiling face I remember. This time, it's a distorted expression, filled with something . . . anger? No, she doesn't look it. What is it? I reach for her, but she's too far. Yet so damn close.

She's mouthing something, but the words are silent. No sounds. Just an image.

"Are you with her, Tia?"

"Yes, she's tired. Sweaty. She's running to my bedroom. Screaming."

"Why? What is she saying?" Another question, but everything blurs, and my head throbs in agony. Then suddenly, piercing sounds. Something screeches. What? I don't know.

My body trembles.

My heart races.

Nothing makes sense.

It's spinning; everything is twirling, making me dizzy.

I can't hear her. *Why can't I hear her?*

"Tia, breathe, listen to my voice." She's trying to calm me, but there's too much happening. *How do I fix it? Momma.* My mind is in turmoil, and my eyes hurt. Tears. I'm crying. *Why am I crying?* "Tia, come back . . . Listen to me. I'm going to count down . . ."

"No! Don't! No!"

"Five."

"Stop!"

"Four."

"Momma, behind you!" I can't leave her. *Why is she making me leave Momma?* Just a moment longer. I can save her. I can get her from the dark. It's so dark. It's red. There's too much red.

"Three."

It's all over me. My hands. The floor. The carpet is stained. The smell is acrid in my nose. Shaking my head, I try to clear my mind. My senses. Everything is too loud. There are people shouting at me. My throat hurts.

"Two."

"NO!" I cry out again, but it's too late. She's gone. I'm gone. They took me away.

"One."

Jolting up, I glance around the room to find her staring at me in horror. My heart thuds so hard it leaves me in pain, breathless, gasping for air. My lungs feel as if they've been punched, kicked. Every time we do this, it's agonizing. But I know I'm closer to finding out what happened that day. I saw it. Some of it. The horror of the blood. So much fucking red. If only I saw where it came from, how it came to be.

"What happened?" I ask, fear dripping from my voice. But all she does is stare at me. "Did I say anything? You have to tell me!" Just then, the clock dings loudly, telling me my time is up. My body is sweaty and shivering.

"I need to study this. I . . . I've never seen anything like it." That's all she tells me before escorting me out of her office.

the past

braxton

Since I left Tia's apartment, I've been focused on doing a background check on her. As much as I enjoyed last night, I'm more intrigued to learn about the woman she is. Or was. When she's silent, something screams to me, as if in her mind she's calling for help, and I intend on doing just that.

Her demeanor, everything about her, has me bewitched. But there's something else. It's like when she's with me, she goes somewhere. Her focus is faulty. It reminds me of those moments where I'm driving on a long road, listening to my favorite song, when suddenly, the frequency fucks out, and I'm listening to static.

She's broken, so fucking broken.

As much of an asshole as I normally am with women, with her I'm different. I want to treat her right and show her how incredible she is and to piece her back together. The thought jolts me, causing me to shake my head to clear the thoughts running rampant in my mind.

"Hey man, you look like you've been deep inside some tight, hot pussy," Grant grunts as I walk up to the entrance of our headquarters. He's lugging a delivery through the door when he gives me a sideways glance.

"Shut it." Stalking past him, I enter the warehouse and head straight for the office upstairs. I'm not late, which is a fucking miracle. When Tia let me sit her on the counter in the bathroom to eat that sweet pussy, I was a goner.

"Braxton, come in. Nice to see you're on time." Corp sits back and regards me as I saunter into his office. He reminds me of my father—strict and controlling. Even though I hated it while growing up, now I look back and realize he was only trying to teach me to be a good man, to work hard and never give up.

"I like to surprise you sometimes." Shrugging, I flop onto the chair facing his desk and wait for my partner in crime to arrive. "So, this club. It's manned by ten security guards. I counted them last night. And there's also video cameras in each corner."

He nods, pulling out the folder and perusing quietly through the paperwork. "The owner goes by the name of Miguel. He's a dirty dealer on all counts. We've got the drug dealing, the money laundering, and the girls being sold, although we don't know if it's into the slave trade in China, or if they're sending them to Thailand to brothels. There have, however, been reports of well-known syndicates set up where wealthy men go to bid on girls. Highest bidder wins." He lifts his steel-gray eyes to me, and they're swirling with anger and frustration.

This has been a job that's been on the back burner because of all the urgent ones we've had come in, but this time, I'm making it my life's mission to get this fucker and burn him to the ground. "We can do this." My adamant tone earns me a rare smile.

"That's why I like you, Cart—" Corp's words are interrupted by Ryker barreling in through the door. He flops into the seat beside me and regards us both with his bloodshot eyes.

"Ryker Murphy, to what do I owe this pleasure?" Corp questions with pure venom in his tone, but the man I called my best friend, the man I've known my whole life, doesn't even flinch.

"You called, I arrived. Let's do this." The air thickens with tension I can cut with a knife.

"I suggest you go and sleep off whatever the hell it is that's wrong with you. When you figure out what it is you want to do, then you can return. Other than that, I do not want you on my property looking like you've been dragged along the street by an assailant and dropped off at my door."

Corp is stern, he's strict, and when he talks, you listen. He pins Ryk with a glare that most men, including me, would cringe under, but when the man beside me rises, he smirks and pivots, stumbling into a small wooden table beside him, toppling it over with a loud crash. "You best get that, pretty boy Carter, since everyone seems to love you."

The stumbling man I no longer recognize leaves, and I'm left dumbfounded. We've been friends for so many years. I've forgiven him for so much, but today, that was the last straw. There's only so much you can do for a man. If he keeps pushing you away, there's nothing you can do but let him figure out his demons.

I've watched him unravel over the years. I've seen him break and shatter before me. And every time I tried to help, to be there, he'd push and push. My best friend is no longer the man I grew up with.

"I'm reassigning you a partner," Corp says immediately, his gaze burning into me with curiosity, probably wondering what just happened. I nod. There's nothing I want more right now. "You'll work with Grant. He's heading out into the field for the first time, and I think you're just the man to show him how it's done. Also, he's got a good head on his shoulders." With that, he picks up the phone on his desk and dials. "Get up here now."

Suddenly, my world tilts on its axis. Everything is changing, and I remember my father's advice in this moment. It's an unbidden memory, and when it hits me, I feel breathless.

"When you leave, go with your morals, your confidence, and that heart that seems to love easily. And when you come back, make sure you bring those same things back with you. Don't let what you see there change you, and don't ever let it diminish the man I taught you to be." I regard my father. The pride glowing in his eyes warms me.

My mother steps up behind me, wrapping her arms around my waist. The love pours from her, seeping into me, and I know that I'm lucky. I've always been lucky. "Brax, please come back to us. I need you. Promise me you'll come back," she implores me, and I turn in her arms, encircling her in mine. Her body is small. She's frail from years of treatment, but she's still going.

I'm only twenty-one, and they're both already in their early sixties. They had me late in life, a miracle son they'd tried for, and when I finally arrived, they smothered me with so much love, so much joy, and everything a boy could need. As I grew older, it was a matter of giving back, and I did. I worked hard and paid my way from a young age. Now, looking at them, I realize I was truly blessed.

"I'll see you soon, Mom." Planting a soft kiss on the top of her head, I give her one last cuddle before turning to my father, shaking his hand, and walking out the door with my backpack ready for war.

"What's up, Corp?" Grant stalks in, and I'm sure I feel the ground beneath me rumble.

"You're partnering up with Braxton. I need you two in that club tonight. Scope it, and I mean every fucking nook and cranny. I want the report on my desk tomorrow, zero nine hundred."

We both nod, and I push up off the chair. I head out to my desk, and Grant follows me. Stopping short of the large wooden table, he regards me with an easy smirk. "What?" I grunt, pulling my chair aside and flopping into it.

"Does he know about your little crush?" He lifts his chin, gesturing at Ryk's desk two down from mine. I nod, waiting for the speech he's about to give me. "All I have to say is, be careful. He's a loose cannon, and you know how dangerous those fuckers are." He turns to walk away, but before he leaves, he glances back at me. "Just watch your back."

I've been around men like them my whole life, people who have been through the ringer, Tia included. My mind drifts back to her often, even when she was dating Ryker. There was always something about her, as if she were a magnet, me a fragment of metal, and I can't keep away.

the present

braxton

Memories.

They're always taunting me. My dreams were filled with images I want to forget.

They were killed. Murdered.

He was my best friend.

I've lost everything.

I only have one thing I cherish. One thing I hold close to my heart.

Her.

The raven-haired, blue-eyed beauty.

It's not just my cock that craves her. My heart does too. I don't know why or how, but she's found that sliver of light in my darkness, and she's placed herself there, burrowing herself deep. She's my salvation. I can't offer her the same because I'm her damnation. I don't see how we'll survive this.

The sun filters through the barred windows, and I stare directly at it, hoping it will blind me, so I never have to look at her again. So I don't see the despair in her expression when I tell her it's over. When I confess who I am, or more importantly, what I am.

Will she still want me?

Perhaps not.

Will she look at me with anger and regret?

Yes.

I have no doubt that she'll be hurt. I should let her go now. Today. I should tell her that I'm leaving, and she's going to have to do this on her own. When I walk away, it needs to be a clean break. She'll move on. She'll find someone better. She deserves it.

A good man would do that. He'd allow her to live a life with a man who can give her everything. Not someone who'll take and take and give nothing in return. That's what an admirable man would do. Someone with morals.

Am I that man? No.

When she walks in here in a few minutes, will I let her go? No.

Why? Because I'm selfish. I want to defile her. I want to use her to gain my sanity. I want her body, her mind, her heart, and I'll be damned to hell, but I want her fucking soul. I want to drink it in, basking in its glow. I want to devour everything she has to give. Like a demon feeding on the innocence of a virgin, I want to consume her the way she's consumed me.

The door flies open, and there she is. An angel in the fires of hell.

"I missed you," she murmurs with a smile.

Tell her.

No.

"As I have you." I offer a small nod and rise to my feet, stalking toward her. Her body is hugged by the thin white material of a gown. Her dark nipples tease me as they harden under my scrutiny. "Sit," I order. I turn, gesturing to the bed. Her footfalls are soft, almost silent as she pads over to the small bed in the corner and flops down on it.

Her ice-blue eyes focus on me, and she lifts her legs, crossing them like a kid.

"So, what are we going to play tonight? Do you want to hear the rest of the story?" I question her in a soft murmur, and she nods. I join her on the bed, sitting against the metal headboard and opening my arms to have her nuzzle in them. She curls herself in my grasp as I continue our tale . . .

the past

Tia

"So, you fucked him?" Laney's voice is shrill over the line. I knew she'd be shocked, but I didn't expect her to screech like this.

"Yes, I did. And it was good. I want more, Laney, so much fucking more, and I can't have it." Sighing, I open the door to the bar and step inside. The stale smell of beer hits me. I have to hold my breath as I enter and shut the door behind me with a soft click.

"You'll have to tell him, Tia. If you're going to do this, he needs to know." She's right, but I can't tell him. I cannot bring myself to utter the words. If he knew how messed up I am, he'd walk away so fast my head would spin.

"I have to go. I'll call you tonight." Without waiting for her response, I hang up and make my way behind the counter to stash my purse away in the office behind the bar. The place is eerie when it's closed; a cold shiver runs down my back.

Please don't. Please.

Fucking whore. You'll hurt him.

No, I won't. He's a nice guy.

You've got blood on your hands.

It's over. I can't do this anymore.

Shaking my head, I shut my eyes, rubbing my hands over my face and inhaling a deep breath. My phone buzzes in my pocket, and when I pull it out, I see a message from Brax.

Braxton: *Last night wasn't the last. Care for another dose of me?*

Sighing loudly, I sit back and wonder how this will ever work. It won't. There's no way I can be with anyone. I can't get attached, because as much as I want to deny it, I can't. There will be blood.

You're not worthy. Perhaps he should play with me.

"No."

Yes, I'll milk that dick of his.

"Leave me alone. You're not getting him." I hit reply and tap out a message, but the words aren't right, and before I have time to stop her, she sends it.

Tia: *If you can handle my crazy, I'll handle your dick.*

"Shit! Why?"

Because he's mine too. We're the same, don't you realize that by now? I'm in you, forever.

Rising to my feet, I leave my phone on the counter and walk out of the back office. My head hurts, a dull ache which throbs behind my eyes, and I know I'm about to lose it. Before I get to the main entrance, I feel it, the familiar ache. I drop to my knees.

Gripping the carpet below my hands, I dig my fingers in painfully, hoping it will stop what's about to happen, but everything goes black.

"This is beautiful. Look, Tatiana," my mother's voice calls to me, and I find her smiling back at me holding the dress. She's beautiful. She always has been. There's a light that shines from her.

"I don't want pink, Momma." My whiny voice is loud, and the other people around us turn to look at us with scorn. People are mean. They're horrible. Every day, I have to hide away. They don't like me

because we're different. I want to run away. If we leave, I won't have to be at school with those kids.

"Come on, Tia," she pleads in a softer tone, and I know she's embarrassed by the people watching. They don't look happy, and I can see they don't like us. I move my head up and down. I can't argue because it will only make things worse and have more people looking at us.

When we've finally paid, I walk a few feet in front of her toward the car. The ride home is silent, and I fidget with my skirt. I didn't want this either. She always makes me wear things I don't want.

"I just didn't want pink. It's so girly, and you know how the kids at school are." She doesn't respond when we pull into the driveway. Nothing is said when we go into the house, so I head into my bedroom and lie on my bed.

A pain in my head starts suddenly, and I cry out, clutching at my hair, pulling it from its roots, but it doesn't dull the agony searing through me. Shutting my eyes, I hear my mother's voice, dripping with concern. "Tia, baby, what's wrong? Tia."

When I open my eyes, I see it. Ruby red. No, it's darker. The color is almost black.

The smell is gross. Harsh.

There's so much on the floor.

Blood. Thick dark fluid pooling around the body.

The beautiful dress she was wearing is torn, and I try to cover her up.

An unnatural scream echoes around me.

I wonder where it would be coming from. Another and another. My face is wet.

My eyes spill tears down my cheeks, and I realize I'm the one screaming. My throat burns.

Hands are on my shoulders, pulling me back, but I fight them. I kick and scream, but it's no use, they're too strong.

People rush to my mother's body. I can't stop them.

"NO! Let me go!"

I'm wailing loudly, but the man holding me coos in my ear, "It's okay, little one. Close your eyes. Let your mind wander from here. Think of somewhere else." His words seem to hypnotize me, seeping into my mind as if he's dripping them onto my skin, drop by drop.

I obey and shut my eyes, pushing the horror from my mind, and I picture it. I imagine a world without the pain in my heart. I don't see red, but green. Beautiful fields, sunshine warm on my face.

You'll be okay, I'm here now, *she says. I don't know her, but I like her. She's warm. I need her. The feeling only grows as I'm carried away from the gruesome scene. She's going to be my friend now.*

"Tia!" A deep rumble and my body being jostled has me cracking my eyes open. Deep blue eyes stare down at me. My gaze darts around in alarm. *Shit.* It happened again.

"I'm fine, I'm fine." I push his hand away. Aiden looks at me like I've lost my mind. Unfortunately, that happened a long time ago.

"What the fuck, Tia?" His concern is palpable, but I ignore his question. I can't answer him. Nobody can know about me, about *her.*

He's pretty. No.

Glancing back at the barman, I offer a smile. "I'm good. I think I'm just hungry and felt faint. Get ready to open." I don't wait for his response, turning and heading into the office. Shutting the door behind me, I slump into the chair and hang my head. The ache is gone, but the memory is back with a vengeance. My mother's murder has been filed as a cold case.

It's been nearly seventeen years. They've been filled with agonizing pain. My phone dings, dragging my attention back to the present. Picking it up, I find a reply from Brax.

Braxton: *Crazy I can deal with if you're willing to tell me where you go in that mind of yours, Vixen.*

Tell me your secrets.

I stare at the words for so long my eyes tear up, and when they start to blur, I blink, allowing them to fall, wishing they could wash my past away and allow me a present that's worth living for. But my life is still tainted. No matter how much of my history gets purified, I've still got demons.

Secrets.

The downfall of who I am, of what I am, of the things I've done. Before I can reply, my phone rings. "Hello," I whisper, and I don't know why.

"You're awfully quiet. Did I scare you off when I asked about your secrets?" he quizzes me with a hint of amusement.

"No, I'm at work. I didn't see your message."

Lies. They fall so easily from my mouth.

They stain my life, blackening my soul. But it's the only way I know how to ensure my safety. And the safety of everyone around me.

"Do you realize your voice changes when you tell me something that's so clearly not true?" His words stop my heart; anxiety hits me hard, knocking my breath from me.

"What?"

"I'm trained to read people, Vixen, and you

are an open book to me. Every line, every word you hide behind those blue eyes, behind that beautiful face, and in that chaotic mind."

My world tips on its axis, and dizziness hits me. He can't know. He shouldn't know. "I . . . You're . . ."

"Vixen, let me in. Please! I'm not going to scare off so easily. I've seen wars. I've fought battles. And I'm still here. You, my sweet girl, are nothing compared to what I've been through."

Each word warms me. I want to believe him. I want to bask in him and the sweet promises he utters. But I'm not sweet. I'm broken.

"Look, Braxton, you're being nice—"

"Fuck nice, Tia. I don't want to be nice. I'm not a nice guy, and if you say it, I'll drive down there right now, I'll bend you over that fucking bar counter, and I'll shove my dick so deep inside you that you'll feel me in your goddamn throat."

A loud gasp from my lips has him groaning in response. "You're an asshole."

"Yes, I am. I'm going to get inside your mind, Vixen. The same way I'm going to climb into your body. I'm going to make you come so hard you'll forget your limitations, your barriers you like to keep up. I'll break them down. I'm not scared. I'll see you later." With that, he hangs up, leaving me gaping at the blank screen wondering what the fuck just happened.

the past
braxton

As soon as I hang up, I sit back and stare at the screen in front of me. I've been searching all day, but nothing has come up on the name I have for her. *Tatiana Nunez*. Other than some sixty-year-old woman who died recently.

"What are you up to?" Ryk flops onto the seat beside my desk and leans in to read my screen. "You still hooked on that pussy? She's a fucking head case man. Be careful." He chuckles, punching me on the shoulder like we're best friends, but now, I feel so far removed from him.

Yes, I've known him since we were children. We grew up in each other's homes, but something changed in him, and I don't know him anymore. My best friend is gone, and right now, I don't think I want him back. The man before me has turned into someone I don't recognize.

"What happened to you, man?" I voice the question that is playing in my mind and stare at him. I don't expect an honest answer, but he meets my gaze while pushing off the chair.

"I grew the fuck up, I went to war, and I saw things that changed me, things that can never be unseen. And I'll never be okay again. Now, unless you're going to tell me we're heading out tonight to get some sweet ass, then I suggest you shut the fuck up."

I rise to meet him at my full height. "I was there, I went through everything you did, and if you haven't forgotten, I'm still me. Remember the kid you grew up with? That's me. I didn't turn into a dick."

My retort has him flinching, but he once again meets my indignant stare, and with a dark smirk on his lips, he bites back, "Well, you didn't lose everything when you left. You always had everything, didn't you, pretty boy?" With a final glare, he pivots and leaves me raging beneath the calm exterior I plaster on my face.

"Carter, can I see you?" Corp's deep rumble drags me back to the present.

I nod, stalking to his office; I watch him shut the door behind me.

"Sit." He gestures to the chair I was in only

hours ago.

"I'm sorry about that." My apology comes easily. There's nothing that I'd let jeopardize this job, especially my ex-best friend.

"Look, I'm not sure what happened with you boys, but if he's feeling like the world owes him shit, he won't listen to you. You're a good man, Carter, but if you keep pushing him, he may jump." His earnest advice startles me. He's never been one to give us fatherly advice. Yes, he's in charge of the team, but this feels different.

"He's angry about his girlfriend leaving him. He's been fucking around on her for months, and she finally realized it. Now, he's blaming her." He nods in understanding, then shocks me when he sits back, lifting his fingers into a steeple in front of his mouth, reminding me of a pastor once he's heard a confession.

"And you're interested in her?" he demands.

"No, of course not." I shrug. Yes, I'd like to fuck her into next month, but anything more is out of the fucking question. "It's just that there's something about her . . . She's hiding something. She's got too many secrets, and I want to uncover them. I want to—"

"Save her?" he questions, and I nod easily because I do. "Braxton." My name sounds foreign when he says it. He's never called me by my first name before. "I get where you're coming from, but you can't save everyone, son. There are times you need to let them save themselves. Perhaps you can be her support, but until she lets you in, you can't do shit. You can't force her to tell you what she hides. Maybe those things are what she needs to let go of to move on."

"I understand what you're saying, but surely, I can help her through whatever it is," I implore him, begging him to see my side of this. Needing him to realize that somehow this girl has woven herself into my mind and heart. She's overtaken so much of my thoughts I feel as if it was me who's been with her all these months and not Ryker.

"What did you have in mind?" Resignation is all over his face as he leans forward, waiting for me to confess that I've already been using our software to trace her background. Sighing, I glance at the bookshelf behind him, unsure of my plan. I didn't think it through. "Look, Braxton, we can find out what you need, but I want you to do it by the book."

Snapping my gaze to his, I nod. "I have her name, but somehow, nothing's come up on my searches."

"Can you get me a Social Security number? Perhaps her full name? Do you know that the one she's using is actually hers?"

If she trusts me, then I can find out all I need to do a thorough search.

"I can get the intel, but it will be difficult. She's already wary of me," I confess.

"Sounds like you have a little spitfire on your hands. Come to me when you have more, and I'll see what I can do."

With that, I push up and head to the door. Before I walk out, I turn to him and offer him a salute. "Thank you, Corp, it means a lot." Not waiting for a response, I shut the door behind me and head out to my desk.

"You ready?" Grant saunters up to me; his big bulk moves quickly.

I nod. Grabbing my jacket, I rise and shrug it on. With my keys and phone in hand, we head out to the car.

"So, are you ready to take this asshole down?" my partner questions, his expression serious.

"Yeah, the sooner the better. Sounds like he's got his hands in way too much shit, and he needs to go away. For a very long time." Slipping into the driver's seat, I start the engine and pull out of the driveway.

"I'd like to make sure he goes away permanently." A dark chuckle from my new partner has me nodding in agreement. I'd like to put him away too, six fucking feet underground.

"Yeah," I murmur in response.

The ride from HQ isn't long, and when we pull up outside the bustling club, there's already a queue reaching around the building. Women in the skimpiest fucking clothes I've ever seen stand shivering in the chilly evening air, and I wonder just what is going to happen to them tonight.

A nauseating sensation fills my mind, because I don't want to know. I've already seen too much since working with Retribution, and this sadly is nothing new. "Let's get in there, man. I don't want to spend the whole night out here." Grant's already out of the car before I have time to clear my mind.

The memory of Tia being here dressed like she was sends a wave of frustration through me. She could have been hurt, or worse, she could be one of the girls we rescue from a fucking cage.

Nearing the door, I notice the bouncer giving

us the once-over. Grant gives him a nod, and we're let in through the double-door entrance. As soon as I step inside, the music hits me like a punch to the gut. The bass booms through the speakers, and we're fighting our way through swaying bodies.

Everyone looks as if they've been drinking for much longer than is necessary, and as my gaze darts around, I wonder if any of the patrons—who all look too young to be in a nightclub—know what really goes on here. *Of course they do. Why else would they be here? For the drugs? The girls?*

"Hey man, I'm going to check out the top floor. You okay on your own?"

I settle myself on a stool at the bar. "I'm not twelve. I can take care of myself." As soon as he leaves, I order a beer. The crowd is filled with youngsters, anywhere between eighteen and twenty-five, and suddenly, I feel old.

This used to be my life, before I made something of my future. I wanted to be more than just another one of those kids who woke up ten years down the line and realized that I fucked up.

Sipping my cold beer, I watch the movement around the club, noticing the bouncers and security, until my eyes land on a familiar looking brunette up in the balcony area, talking to an older man. Something about him sets alarm bells ringing in my head.

My hackles rise, and I want to stalk over there and find out what the fuck is going on, but I've learned observation is best. Sit back and watch your opponent before you strike so they don't see you coming, but you know all their moves. Her long hair swishes as she shakes her head in response to whatever the man has said. I can't see her face, but I'm almost certain I know who it is.

Taking another long swig of my drink, I feel heat on my back, and when I turn, there's a pretty little blonde smirking at me. "And what can I do for you?" I question with a grin of my own.

"Just checking out the talent," she murmurs. Her scent, so different from Tia's, makes my stomach roll. *What the fuck is wrong with me?* Normally, I'd be balls deep in this little minx, but right now, all I can think about is the brunette who's talking to our mark, and she's got a vault I'd like to open . . . Her mind.

My focus is on them. She doesn't know I'm here. She hasn't noticed me yet, but I'll keep my eye on her until I know she's safe. Until she's away from that asshole and in my fucking arms.

the present
Tia

"Do you want to try going under again? Regression?"

I shake my head swiftly while watching the rain dance along the windowpane. It's as if it's weeping for me. Tears silently fall, burning my cheeks and eyes at the same time. Everything hurts today. My head, my heart. How do I live like this? I guess I'm used to the throbbing agony. It's become a part of me now.

"It didn't work the last time, or the time before that," I point out calmly, but inside of me there's a war waging.

I'm on the battlefield.

Knives drawn.

Guns blazing.

Two sides to every fight, one has to be the loser. I just wonder who it will be this time.

I've been doing it for so long that I don't recall a time where I didn't want to fight.

Myself.

Others.

Anyone who stood in my way.

"Look, I know this is difficult—" she starts, but halts when I turn to regard her angrily.

"You don't know anything. This"—my index finger prods my temple—"is damaged. Has been for a long time." I lean back, taking a deep breath and trying to calm the frustration.

"I know. Your father—"

"Do. Not. Talk about him," I hiss the words, but she doesn't flinch. Instead, she eyes me warily, waiting. She's always waiting. "I'm not here to talk about him today. You told me you'd help me. That you'd be able to tell me what happened to my mother."

"If you don't want to do regression, we can do hypnosis. It's the only way I can get into your mind, Tia. Do you want to remember that day? What if it's something that will hurt you?"

She's right, but I need to know. *Did I kill my mother?* All my life, I've believed it. Every moment, every day, all my dreams, nightmares. Everything.

"Yes, I need to know."

She nods, her pencil poised. Waiting, watching. Fuck. Always. Her gaze probes me. As if she's boring a hole in my mind, waiting for the memories to seep from my skull like blood.

Red.

Crimson.

The lifeforce that we all need, but it's so easily taken away. Yes, I know how to bleed a man out. I know how to bathe in the liquid and revel in the pungent metallic scent.

"Tia," she says, startling me from the thoughts running rampant through my deluded mind. I meet her gaze and see the sadness in her eyes.

"I can't do that today. Can we talk about something else? Do you think I'll ever have a normal life?" I think I asked her this before. I want a life. With Braxton. I wish we could have kids too. Even if the thought is painful, the idea of him inside me, marking me with his seed and my body accepting it makes me smile. To be pregnant with his babies would be incredible. Sadness taints my grin.

"You can, Tia, but you need to find your anchor. You need to find it and hold on. Do not run into that place inside your mind. Once you stop running, once you don't need that as an escape, that's when you'll be able to have a normal life. You need to face your fears head on."

Her voice is filled with urgency, sincerity, and fear. She's scared I'll always be like this. So am I. And I know Braxton is as well. I don't blame them. It's difficult. *Can I actually do it? Find an anchor?* Yes, Braxton is my anchor. *Isn't he?*

the past
Tia

He's going to hurt you, and you're going to make him bleed.

"No, no, no!" My voice is shrill, echoing through my empty apartment. The throb, a dull ache in my head, makes my eyes blur.

Little Tia, little liar. Broken girl. Did you know broken girls are dirty? No man will love them.

"Leave me alone!" Gripping my ponytail, I pull it loose and massage my temples in small circles. I need my medication, the pills that get me through this.

Let him come. I want to play. I want to feel him. Deep and hard.

Isn't that what you like, Tia?

Remember how it felt being taken roughly by him?

Almost violently?

How good it was?

Ignoring the mind games, I stalk into the kitchen and grab a beer and the small white bottle. My mind is still on the earlier phone call and Brax's adamant tone to learn my secrets. Drowning my sorrows as I drop three tablets onto my tongue and swallow the cold alcohol. The stillness hits me like a wave, as it always does when I get home after a shift. Being alone for so long, I've become accustomed to the quiet, but tonight I feel unease creep in.

The desire to run is strong, but I know I can't. I have to finish what I started. Before I make it to my bedroom, my phone buzzes, and as soon as I look at the screen, my heart leaps into my throat. He's got too much control over me already, and it's only been one night.

But the peace he gave me makes me want more, crave more. Swiping my finger over the screen, I answer, yearning to hear his voice. "Hello, Carter." Using his last name, I stifle a giggle when he groans loudly.

"Vixen." His voice is low, breathy, and sends a jolt directly to my core. "I'm outside. I suggest you open up." The words and promise of being around him has me trembling with excitement. Heading to the door, I unlock it and pull it open.

"You'll need the elevator code."

"Well . . .?"

I giggle at his insistence. "It's three five seven two eight, and the door is open." I head into the kitchen with him still on the line. Pulling out two bottles of beer from the refrigerator, I place them on the countertop. "Are you close?"

"I am." His voice echoes from the line to the door, and when he steps into the apartment, my breath hitches. Dressed in a dark blue button-up and ripped black jeans that hug his muscular thighs, he has me salivating. "You look lovely," he murmurs in that deep, seductive growl which ignites heat all over my skin.

A slow perusal starts from my feet. He trails his gaze up my legs, hips. Those caramel eyes blazing when he notices my hard nipples. He inches his stare to my mouth, and when he finally meets my eyes, they're molten.

"Do I?" I quip, tipping my head to the side. The ache in my skull from my earlier episode dissipates as he nears me. His hands grip my hips, tugging me against him.

"You do, Vixen. Good enough to eat." His words are a reminder of this morning's *goodbye* before he left for work. "Would you like that, baby?" he coos in my ear, running his nose up the side of my neck, inhaling my scent. "Jesus, you smell good. Makes my cock hard."

"Does it now? Did you only come here to fuck me? Or is there some other reason you're standing in my kitchen?" My voice is raspy with need as I trail my fingernail down the buttons of his shirt. The material hugs his shoulders, and I wish I were draped over him so closely.

I want to wrap myself around his body, inside his very soul. To connect myself to him so the pain eases. So that *she* doesn't come back.

"I did come here to fuck you, to drive into you, and make you cry out my name, but before we get there, we're going to talk." He leans in farther, pressing his soft lips to the nape of my neck in a featherlight kiss. My skin tingles at the contact, making me dizzy with an ache deep in my belly. "Did you like that, Vixen?" he questions against the sensitive skin.

"Maybe," I tease, but when he steps back suddenly, I see questions upon questions swimming in his gaze.

"Is this for me?" He grabs a bottle, handing me the other, and I nod. "Let's sit." The way he seems to take charge makes me feel safe, like he'd be able to cure me. To take away the demons plaguing me.

Once we're seated in the living room, my legs curled under me and my bottle in hand, I watch him intently. The air in the room is thick with tension, but he tries to hide it.

It's strange how people's eyes hold so much. They think they've got a stoic expression, but their gaze speaks volumes. It shouts and screams at me. It reminds me of a day when I finally realized that what you see on the outside is not what's hidden beneath.

"Tell me, Vixen? What is it that hides beneath that pristine exterior?"

Turning my attention to Brax, I watch him for a moment before sipping my beer. I never used to enjoy the taste, but slowly, I've grown to love it, and somehow, this seems to be getting me through.

"I'm a girl from a broken home. I've been on my own for years. There's not much to me, Braxton. You're making a mountain out of a molehill. And do you know what they say about curiosity and the cat?" I quirk my mouth.

His eyes crease at the sides when a breathtaking smile plays on his full mouth. His lower lip is more prominent than the top, but they're incredible. Feeling them on my body is like detonating a bomb — explosive.

Don't get attached.

"Fuck," I bite out in frustration. Pushing off the sofa, I place the bottle on the table and walk over to the window. The city below twinkles in the dark, but I know in that gloominess lies secrets—dark secrets. Vile and disgusting things people do that make me shudder.

I feel him before he reaches me, as if we're magnetized. Soft, warm hands grip my shoulders; it's not a commanding hold, rather a reassuring one.

Something inside me stills, waiting for him to make the next move.

You see, I'm trained now. I'm no longer a helpless little girl. So, if I'm ever threatened, I know how to defend myself. "I have so many questions for you, Vixen, but the first one is the most important. Why do you push me away?" The question fans over my heated skin. It prickles with yearning, with desire, with need for him, but I don't let him see my resolve, my submission. My body is still, my gaze focused on the lights that hide the immoral acts that happen below me.

"Because it's easier." The raspy tone in my answer is evidence of his effect on me. It's clear that my feelings for this man may be my downfall.

Even though I ache for him to be my salvation, I don't know for sure if he'll save me.

"That's not an answer. You need to be honest with me," he implores, his tone ragged and gruff in my ear, sending more heat skittering over my fevered skin.

"And what makes you think I'm going to be honest with you, Braxton? My life isn't all fucking sunshine and rainbows."

"I didn't say it was. Mine is far from that. I'm not expecting you to tell me everything tonight, but if this" — he spins me around and gestures between us — "is going to work, you'll need to talk to me. You'll need to open up and let me in at some point because I'm not going to run away."

"Braxton, please, just stop. Don't ask me something you don't need or want the answers to." Pushing away from him, I stalk into the kitchen and grab another beer.

"Jesus, Tia, let me in!" His growl is right behind me, and when I pivot, his body is close. Too close.

"Get out!" My words echo around us, but he doesn't listen. Gripping my hips in a viselike hold, he lifts me against his body and walks us backward until my body is flush with the fridge. I'm pinned between his solid torso and the cool metal on my back.

"I will not leave you. You want to fight. Let's fight. Come on, slap me, curse me, do what you want, but I'm not letting you go." The low, dangerous tone of his voice has my body pulsing with animalistic need. "You can't do it, can you? Come on, Vixen," he taunts, "you want me to hurt you? I'll give you the best angry fuck you've ever had, and after that, you'll answer every goddamn question."

Without another word, he reaches for my jeans and unbuttons them, shoving them down my legs. His fingers tug the skimpy material of my thong, ripping it from my body. A gasp falls from my lips, and he gifts me a sexy smirk. "Brax," I whimper, his name a moan, a prayer.

He doesn't respond with words, and when I feel him impale me, I let out a mewl so soft and tender my body shudders. "That's right, Vixen, you want to claw me, scratch me? Fucking do it. Because the only way I'll hurt you is by fucking you raw."

the past

braxton

My growl shudders through her slim frame as she trembles at my words. The slick heat taunts me as I slide into her body. It's incredible. Long, manicured nails dig into my shoulders, just as I asked, as I commanded her to do. I've been gentle when we've been together, but today, that's out the window.

I plunge into her tightness. "You" — thrust — "feel" — thrust — "this?" Her head bobs as she tries to nod. "This is me fucking you." My hips slam her against the fridge violently. This isn't sweet lovemaking; this isn't even fucking; this is basal, a primal connection.

Her piercing blue orbs pin me with a heated glare. Hatred, anger, venom swirl like a maelstrom, and I don't care because I know those emotions aren't for me. She's fighting something, warring against her past, which I'm about to drive right out of her with my dick buried deep in her tight little cunt.

"Oh, God!" she cries out, and I know she's tumbling into the abyss. Her pussy clamps down on my cock, and I feel her arousal soaking me. My body trembles, and my orgasm skitters down my spine, my grip on her fierce, and I realize I'm probably bruising her, but I can't stop.

Our bodies find euphoria together as I grunt one final time before emptying myself inside her. "Jesus, Tia, you'll kill me," I murmur against her neck. Her languid body molds to me, and her arms twine around my neck, pulling me closer as if I'm her lifeline and she's washed away at sea. "Is that what you wanted, baby? To be fucked, rough and hard?" I question, placing a tender kiss on her lips.

"I just want to forget, and you keep asking me to remember."

Her confession stills me, and her ice-blue eyes seem to melt. "I want you to trust me."

Shaking her head, she lowers her legs. Her feet touch the floor, and she's already letting me go. As soon as our bodies are apart, the cold freezes me. Tucking myself back into my jeans, I zip them up and regard her as she tugs on her jeans, leaving her ripped panties on the floor. "Trust isn't something easily found in my world."

"Is that why you were at the club tonight? Did you go there to find someone else?"

A wry laugh falls from her plump lips. She lifts the bottle to them, taking a long gulp of the alcohol I'm guessing she's using to calm herself.

"Come on, Tia, do you want me here or not?" Nearing her, I reach out, half expecting her to pull away, but when she stills and allows me to touch her, the ache in my chest eases somewhat. Meeting those intense eyes of hers always sends me reeling, and when I cup her face in my hands, I hold her steady so she has to meet my gaze.

"I don't know what you're talking about. I've been at work, and I came straight here. Perhaps you're seeing me because you're obsessed with me?" she quips, leaving me utterly confused because I'm sure it was her in the club tonight. "And yes, I do want you here, but I need your patience. I need you to let this go and stop pushing. Stop forcing me." There's rabid emotion behind her words, almost a feral growl. She's adamant, so I nod. If I can get her to trust me first, she'll open up. At least, that's what I tell myself.

"Fine, no more questions. For now," I warn her. "But let's get one thing clear. I'm not letting this go. When you're ready, I'm here." My words are sincere, and I hope she can see the honesty in my eyes. Because nothing I can say will change her mind right now, so I'll bide my time.

It's been a few hours, and I'm still lying wide awake. Sleep evades as it used to so many times before. When I first found my parents, even when I was still in the army, things I saw used to leave my mind racing a million miles a minute.

That's why I never stay the night with any woman. Not that there have been many, but as soon as it's done, I leave. I walk out with no regrets. The idea of having them see what kind of tormented man I am doesn't bode well. So, I pull on my clothes and leave. But with her, Tia, I want to stay. I don't want to leave her alone.

Glancing to the side, I watch her in the dim light of the full moon. Her features glow beautifully. She looks like an angel. I wonder what dark secrets she hides behind those pretty blue eyes.

Her light colored orbs, mixed with her dark skin, are alluring. A beauty like no other I've seen, and I wonder about her parents, her heritage. I find myself wanting to know her more intimately than just the sex we've had.

I want to know if she'd take me home to meet said parents. If her father would hate me, and her mother would think I'm good for her. I am. I'm good for her, if only she would see it.

"Watching me sleep is creepy, you know," she says sleepily. Her voice is raspy and sexy. Her eyes flutter open, and she regards me with a small smile on her full lips.

"It's the only time I get to really see you," I respond, my voice low. I scoot deeper into the bed and tug her onto my chest. Her body is warm; her skin feels like silk, smooth and soft.

"Why do you want to get inside my mind so much, Braxton? What if you find something you don't like?" She lifts her head and watches me.

"Tia, I'm not the easiest person to be with. I have ghosts and demons that haunt me on a daily basis. But, if you asked me anything, I'd be honest with you. If you didn't like it, I'd just show you other ways you could like me. A relationship is give and take. I just want to know the woman who seems so intent on hiding herself. I want to learn what makes you tick, what makes you fly apart, and what makes you want to hold on instead of letting go. You seem very intent on running, but I'm determined to catch you."

She giggles, snuggling farther into my arms. Her finger traces slow circles on my chest, trailing its way down my torso and under the sheet. Her hand grips my hardening cock, and I let out a low, hungry growl. "How about I do this?" She moves down the bed, the sheet is gone, and her mouth engulfs the tip of my shaft.

Warm and wet, her lips wrap around me, swallowing me into her throat. Every. Fucking. Inch. I grip the sheet below, my knuckles white as I nearly tear the material when she hums. Lifting her head, she watches me. Our eyes lock, and her mouth pops off. "My mother is dead," she informs, once again sucking me into her mouth. "My father should be dead." She continues her story between giving me the best blowjob I've ever had and telling me about her family. "I grew up around a lot of hatred." My concentration slips, and my eyes flutter closed. If this is her way of telling me her story, it's not going to work.

Sitting up, I reach for her, pulling her off

my now solid dick. She lets out a sexy yelp as I position her above me. Her heat slowly envelops me as she slides down my shaft. "My parents are both dead, killed by a monster," I tell her as I thrust my hips up into her tight body. "I found them when I got home from my deployment." I drive deeper, hitting that spot I know drives her crazy. She's clawing at my chest, but I don't care. "I've made it my life's mission to find the fucker who did it," I bite out, all the while her body tightens around me. "And I'm going to rip him apart." My hips buck, faster and faster. Her breathing is ragged as she whimpers. Tears roll down her cheeks as I fuck her mercilessly.

"Braxton," she cries out my name as her body convulses.

"That's my Vixen," I coo as I join her in bliss. My release shudders through me at an alarming pace, and my grip on her hips will leave a mark, but I don't care because I want this woman, with everything I am.

the present

Tia

"Did he tell you he loves you?" she asks, and I shake my head quickly. We've never spoken those words to each other; it's been an unspoken truth. Those are the best. Quiet moments with Braxton calm me. They make me feel alive and real, and most importantly, normal. "Then you should tell him. Take the first step. Perhaps you should tell him about our sessions? About your prognosis, just for him to understand."

"No, I can't tell him. He can't know how fucked up I am. I'll lose him." My confession startles me. I've never been scared of losing someone. My feelings have never been an issue for me. But Braxton seems to have cracked my shell. As scary as that is, I want him. He's burrowed himself inside me, and I know I'm falling. *Or have I already fallen?* I can't remember.

I know he's mine. I'm his.

"I think you should talk to him. If you want this long term, you'll need him to understand you." She's right. She's always right. But how do you tell someone you're in love with them?

"And if I want this long term, I don't want him disappearing because I'm crazy. Because I'm broken. Why would he want someone with fragments of her old self? Someone who sometimes can't even remember where she was last night?" Taking a steadying breath, I try to envision what it would feel like if Braxton walked away and left me. *What would I do?* "I can't even give him children. Do you know that? I'm no longer a woman. I can't bear children after what they did to me," I continue harshly, hatred dripping like acid from my lips, burning me as I spew the words. "My father made sure no man would ever love me."

"I know he hurt you, Tia," she coos, but it only angers me further.

"You don't fucking know anything," I bite out, and she flinches. "He fucking ripped me apart. My body is not whole. My heart is not whole. And my mind" — I let out a dark chuckle — "well, you know what my mind is like." My grip on the chair tightens, and I feel my nails digging into the smooth, faux leather.

"Tell me." She sets the notebook on the small table beside her.

"What?"

"Everything, I want to hear everything. I won't note it. I want to look at you while you relive it. Let me experience it with you," she affirms with a nod of her head, and my mouth falls open.

"No."

"Tia, he made you believe what happened to you was your fault. How did he do that?" She tips her head to the side and watches me intently like I'm some kind of animal in a cage.

"He . . ." My words taper off as I try to figure out how the fuck I'm meant to explain it to her. *Can I voice the words?* "When my mother was killed—" Pain slices at my heart, but I take a deep breath and continue. "I mean," I blink away the tears that burn my eyes. "After she was killed..." I take a long inhale, hold it, then exhale. "He told me my sister needed to go away . . . to school . . . That I'd be the woman of the house, and it came with responsibility."

"So, you played mom and wife to him?" Her tone is angry and incredulous, but there's no other way to explain it. She's right. As wrong as it is, that's what I was. I was only thirteen. Yes, deep down, I knew it was wrong, but with the drugs he pumped into me, I had no choice. I was compliant. Just like he wanted.

"Yes," I croak. My throat is about to close and suffocate me. "He gave me a drink every day. It was a clear liquid. Strong and harsh on my young throat, but he told me it was good for me."

"Do you know what it was?"

"I didn't at the time. When I turned eighteen, I escaped and started researching. I found out it was Scopolamine. It's a drug used in Colombia similar to the well-known Rohypnol. Of course, my father had an array of these at his disposal. What Scopolamine does is wear the user down, leaving you with memory loss and sleepiness. You're not able to . . ." I shut my eyes so tight I see white behind the lids as memories assault me. Not real ones though, just flashes, the pain and agony smarting my body.

"You're not able to what, Tia?"

"Not able to fight someone off." I open my eyes to regard her again as the truth falls from my lips. Her mouth gapes in a loud gasp that seems to echo through the room.

"So, he raped you repeatedly." Her

whispered realization has me nodding. "In your mind, it was wrong, but you had no way of doing anything." Again, I assent my agreement in her deductions.

"I was just a girl."

"And his friends, colleagues?"

"They joined in most times. I was homeschooled, so I didn't have anyone I could talk to or ask for help. It was me against him. His power and money spread far in our town. They were strong, cartel, leading the human trafficking rings in the city I grew up in. I didn't have a choice but to wait, to bide my time until I could fight back."

"When you were eighteen."

I nod. "Yes. I ran, packed what I could, stole some money from the safe, and made sure I couldn't be found." My voice is so small, so pained, when I look at her, I see it in her eyes, sadness and compassion.

"You're safe now, Tia." She smiles; it's small but filled with a pity that chokes me.

I shake my head quickly, making myself dizzy with the movement. "I'm never safe. Not until he's dead."

The ding of the clock tells us my time is up for today, so I rise and grab my jacket. Shrugging it on, I make my way to the door. Stifling sadness wraps its claws around my heart as I twist the handle.

"I'm not telling Braxton." It's a promise. I can't tell him. I don't wait for her response; instead, I walk out of the warmth of her office and into the stark, chilly hallway.

He'll never know. I can't lose him. I'll lose everything.

My sanity. My man. My love.

the past

Tia

My gaze meets his. It's dark. Something feral in the way he looks at me has my head spinning ever so slightly. My body quakes, and my heart rate increases. "Why are you here?" Backing away slowly, I don't allow my gaze to stray from him. He doesn't answer me; he never does. I'm afraid that if he stays, I'll hurt him. She'll hurt him. She always hurts them. Men.

"I came to see if you're okay, Tia. You can't live like this." He gestures around him at the vile apartment I'm currently sleeping in, but it's his fault. He found me, and I can't run. My gaze darts around, but there's no way out.

Turning from his intense, almost-black eyes, I watch the sun setting on the horizon. I can't do this anymore. Every time I see him, it's the same thing. I hate him, and he wants me back home.

He's going to pay.

No. Please.

"Get out of my home," I tell him adamantly, but he doesn't listen. They never do. It's as if I'm the one who calls them and begs them to stay. But I don't, *she* does.

"How about we try it another way?" His words are close, and they fan over my neck in a warm breath. Shutting my eyes, I will myself not to respond, for my body not to betray me. "Come on, Tia?" he pleads, his hands on my hips, pressing my ass against the thick erection that's filled me so many times. All those times it's been her, not me. He convinced me, and I allowed it to happen. He broke me, tore me apart, and she let it happen. Only when I finally turned eighteen did I finally walk away, but he found me.

But before I can refuse him this time, he's on top of me. Pressing me into the sofa. A sleek, steel blade comes from nowhere, and he presses it against my neck. Hate burns my veins, coursing through me along with fear.

My muffled cries are drowned out by the music that suddenly blares through the speakers.

Loud. Heavy Metal. Raging music.

I've been here before.

Do you remember? she taunts me.

How could I forget?

Then do something. I taught you how.

She did. Everything I know is because of her. My skin-tight yoga pants get ripped from my body, and tears fall from my eyes, soaking the material of the sofa with my pain and agony. "Look at that pretty pussy. Come on, Tia. I know you like when we do this, when I fuck you hard and raw." His deep growl is venomous. It shudders through me. It's fierce, feral, and it makes me want to rip the skin off his bones. To see his blood stain my hands.

My skin alights with the knowledge of how to stop it, but if I do, he'll never breathe again.

Can I do it?

Yes, do it.

Why? Why doesn't he stop? I question, but she's gone. Leaving me to fend for myself. His hands grip my legs, wrenching them apart.

"Look at you, baby girl, such a sweet little cunt." Before the searing pain of his fingers engulf me, I manage to push off the cushions as the adrenaline courses through my veins. His body jolts upright in shock, and when I meet those dark, animalistic eyes, I see it.

"Fuck you!" I lunge at him; my nails claw the skin of his face, ripping down his cheek as red spills. Thick, coppery scented. I revel in the way it seeps from the wound.

His hands grip my wrists, but I don't give up.

Spitting in his face, I see the rage darkening his eyes further. It's as if I'm staring at the Devil himself. "You'll fucking pay, little bitch." He hisses as my knee comes up, but he anticipates my move, blocking it. He releases his grip on one hand, and without warning, backhands me across the face.

The sting on my cheek burns, blood dripping from my mouth. Another whack, and I'm dizzy. He's too strong. One hand grips my neck, tightening painfully. My body flails in his grasp as he lifts me in the air. The dark cherry red lifeforce trickles from my lips and onto his cheek.

He looks like a warrior in battle, with his opponent's blood adorning him like a victory mask. "How are you so strong, and you're only a waif?" he quips with a sadistic grin. "That's okay, you don't have to answer me," he responds. My choking sounds, mingled with the music, all make for a grim symphony.

Lowering me, he holds me inches from his face.

The face I used to love and trust.

The face of a man I thought I knew.

Now when I look at him, I see evil.

He releases me, and my lungs pull air in sharp bursts. When I drag my gaze to his, I choke out the vow I will keep until I've fulfilled it. "I'll kill you one day, Father."

Jolting upright, I pull in one breath after the other, deeper and deeper, but it feels as if I'm drowning. "Baby?" a voice murmurs from behind me, and a scream is ripped from my throat, but when I turn to see where the rough baritone comes from, I find Braxton, with his sleep-mussed hair and caramel eyes staring back at me.

"What . . .? I . . ."

"You were mumbling in your sleep, and then suddenly, just jerked up. Was it a nightmare? Talk to me, baby?" He reaches out, and instinctively, I pull away, not wanting or needing a man touching me. But when I turn my attention to his face, that handsome face that was buried between my legs only hours ago, I realize he isn't the monster. The pain I'm causing him, the agonizing expression and the wariness he regards me with, cracks the murky, detached shell that is my heart.

"I . . . I need water," I mumble, earning a scowl from him, but I can't tell him about my nightmare. There's no way he'll understand.

"I'll get you some, baby," he soothes, his words calming my erratic heart.

The fact that my nightmare wasn't only

about the last time I saw my father but was also the day I became a person who uses my body to get the answers I need, sent me into a panic.

I went into a depression that I don't think I ever got out of. I did anything and everything I could to find out where he went. He left the apartment I was sharing with some friends and disappeared.

He's coming for you.

No, shut up.

Brax returns carrying a pitcher of water and a glass. "I figured you'd need more than one glass. That scream could have woken the dead." He settles beside me with a calm expression, but in those honey eyes, I see everything playing out like a movie. All his questions and all the concern for a girl he thinks he loves. It's only been a month, but I can see the way he looks at me.

Ryker was different, so vastly different that I couldn't compare the two men. He was never this attentive, and as much as Brax acts like an asshole, I know he's not. Something in his eyes tells me there's a man hurting in there, and I wish I could fix him. But, fuck, I can't even fix myself.

Brax has told me about the snide comments

coming from my ex, the man who was fucking me over for far too long. And now that I've moved on, he's angry. Deranged almost. Thankfully, he hasn't come near me. Fear of that stays with me daily, because I know if he was near me, I'd hurt him. More than I'd like to let on.

"Are you okay? Please talk to me?" His questions sound quietly in the dim light streaming through the window. I normally leave my curtains open, but tonight they're drawn, leaving only a sliver of light coming through. His soft voice is filled with concern. I don't want him to worry about me. He's giving too much, and I'm just taking, grabbing and holding on with both hands. I don't want to let him go. At this point, walking away from Braxton Carter may kill me.

There's no way I can tell him about the nightmare, so I shrug it off and swallow the water he brought. Hoping with everything I am that he'll drop it, but I know he won't. He's stubborn like that.

"Are you always going to ignore me when I ask you something personal?" His murmured question sounds like an alarm in the silence. I chose this apartment because it was private. No other people can get close to me, nor me to them.

"Yes." I turn to place the glass on the nightstand. I shift deeper under the blanket and pull it over me. His silhouette blocks the minimal illumination, which in turn makes him seem as if he were an ethereal being.

An angel.

My savior.

No one can save you, Tia.

the past

braxton

"Let me take you out?" I ask, sipping the beer she's just poured for me. It's been two long days where work has kept me from her. Phone and text messages don't compare to being in her presence or looking into her eyes.

"On a date?" she quizzes in amusement, and I nod. "And where would you take me?"

Sitting back, I regard her through narrowed eyes. "The fair, this Saturday." I shrug, watching shock paint her face with a gorgeous, teasing smile.

"Really?" I nod. "And what makes you think I'll want to go to a fair?"

"From what we confessed the other day, I feel like we need to unwind, just act like teenagers having a laugh and not talk about anything serious. Let's be normal," I offer quietly. My heart leaps into my throat, waiting.

"Okay." She smiles, walking off to serve one of her customers. Her hips sway, taunting and teasing me. She loves to entice me and she does it so fucking well that I'm salivating, aching to drive into her body and show her how much I care for her.

Finishing my beer, I pull out my phone and text Grant. Tomorrow, we're hitting the club and making our move. I want to take that fucker down so fast his head will spin.

"You want another one, Brax?" I'll never tire of hearing her say my name. It's better when she's screaming it, but we'll leave that for later.

"No thank you, Vixen, I need to meet Grant for a quick meeting. I'll see you later?" Meeting her ice-blue gaze, she nods with a smile. Leaning in, I plant a long kiss on her lips. "And I would prefer you in those red lace panties," I whisper along her lips. With that, I turn and leave her staring at my back.

※

The warmth of Tia's body wakes me, and as I roll over, I glance at the beauty beside me. I shouldn't have stayed with her tonight, because as I look at her, my heart fills with emotion.

Jesus, Brax you're turning into a pussy.

Her long, flowing hair fans on the pillow, and those thick eyelashes flutter as she dreams silently.

I must watch her in the darkness for far too long because when I take note of the time, I realize I've been watching her sleep for at least an hour. Her eyes flutter, and she whimpers. It's a soft sound in the room. It's so quiet I could have missed it.

My heart races when she pleads to no one in particular. It's a soft plea to leave her alone. To stop torturing her. If I can find out who haunts her, I can help. If only she'd open up to me. Trust me. Closing my eyes, I lean back on the headboard and calm myself. I try to breathe deeply, allowing my blood to cool.

My nerves are frayed for this woman who has a hold on me.

She consumes me.

Days, weeks, and fucking months, I've wanted her.

Ached for her.

Somehow, I don't know if I can ever let her go, and the thought scares me. I've been in love once. Sure, I've fucked women, but this . . . this is different. I don't consider myself a manwhore because I don't even stay for one night, and I've never considered myself ready for a wife, a family. It's never been in my plan. Sleeping beside a woman is not something I've become accustomed to. The first and last time I did before Tia, it ended in me almost killing her.

I woke from a nightmare of my time in Afghanistan and opened my eyes to find my hands wrapped securely around her slender neck. The same place I had spent hours devouring with my teeth, tongue, and lips. From that day, I vowed never to spend the night beside anyone.

I decided to focus on what I wanted since I arrived back. My plan was to find the man who killed my parents. Or had them killed.

Then Tia walked into my life, crashing into me with her own storm burning in her big blue eyes. A hurricane that I found myself drawn to. I craved to get caught in it and feel the agony and pleasure she promises. She rages and I fight, we fuck, we scream and shout, but through all that, I want to break down those fucking walls.

I push off the bed and take quiet steps into the hallway and listen. I can see the living room from here, and the bright red numbers on her sound system tell me it's two a.m. I follow the lights, hoping to find something while she's still asleep.

I don't want to do this, but I don't have a choice. I find her purse on the sofa and unzip it slowly. The hiss echoes through the cavernous space, and I wait a moment before opening the leather. A small wallet sits inside, beckoning me, and my curiosity wins out.

Opening it, I find her driver's license. The photo is my girl, Tia, but the name on the card is not the one she told me. The name on the card sends me into panic, spiraling into a dark memory.

"Dad, Mom, I'm home!" I call out, dropping my rucksack on the floor in the entrance foyer to my childhood home. I've been released from service because of an injury, and all I've been looking forward to is my mom's homecooked meals and my dad's advice on what to do now.

He's been there for me through everything, and I know he's been trying to get me a job with a security firm since I told them I'm coming home. The house is silent as I stalk my way around the lower level. Frowning in confusion at the lack of response, I head upstairs and push open the familiar door at the top of the landing.

Everything from my teenage bedroom greets me. I should've figured Mom wouldn't give anything away. Perhaps they've gone out, but I decide to check the rest of the house before heading back out. "Mom? Dad?" I push into the bedroom, and everything I've had in my stomach comes flying out.

Blood.

Red.

Everywhere.

The iron stench burns my nostrils; tears sting my eyes as their lifeless bodies blur. My heart aches. The agony leaves me breathless, and I drop to my knees. Gripping the carpet beneath my fingers, I fist my hands, tugging the soft gray wool, ripping it from the floor. A loud, agonizing cry is torn from my throat. Not one, not two, but three screams later, my throat burns as if there's a fire blazing through it.

I don't know who did this, but they'll pay. With their own fucking life.

I will find them, tear them to pieces, and watch as their blood stains my hands.

They'll beg and cry for mercy, but I'll show none.

Shoving her wallet back into the small leather bag, I swallow the anger that seems to be bubbling up inside. My blood heats as my mind tries to make sense of what I've just found out.

Alvarez, not Nunez. Why would she lie? Why would she change her name?

Unless she knows who I am, my past?

Possibilities run rampant as I reach for the alcohol and tumbler. Pouring a double shot, I quickly down it and refill my glass. The burn of the amber drink alleviates the frustration, but it doesn't stop the rage that burns, licking at me like a flame, threatening to engulf me.

I head toward the large windows that overlook the city, taking in the bright lights below. The darkness steals its way across the buildings, and the silver illumination of the full moon hanging in the sky is the only thing that offers natural light.

I've spent many nights wondering what I'd do when I found him—the man who killed my parents. It was something I'd vowed to do and seek revenge for what he did.

After the fateful day I found them, we discovered my father had turned down an offer to pick up a case where the felon was facing an attempted murder conviction. The lawyer in my dad didn't believe in the case and didn't want to represent someone he felt was guilty.

We didn't think anything of it. My father had turned down many cases in the past, but this particular one was what changed our lives. The man in question, Miguel Alvarez, had been released on good behavior. Now we can't find the fucker. All these years I've searched for my parents' killer and always come up emptyhanded.

"You okay?" Tia's sultry voice comes from behind me. Her bare breasts press against my naked torso as she snakes her arms around my waist. I need to play this right. She can't know that I know who she is. I need to figure out how to get into her head and find out why she's here, in my life.

She's the key to her father, so I twist in her arms and down my bourbon, setting the glass on the table at the window. Encircling her in my grasp, I tug her body against mine, feeling the stirring of my cock when her nipples pebble against my chest. "I'm fine. Just thinking about how I'd like to fuck you next. Maybe I should tie you to your bed and have my wicked way with that sweet little pussy." Her eyes glow with something other than desire.

"No. I don't like being tied up." She tries to step away, but I hold onto her.

"Then I'll just bend you over and eat you out from behind. I'd lick my way from that tiny clit all the way to your sexy ass," I growl in her ear, and the responding shudder makes me smile.

"I can handle that," she murmurs playfully, but something about this demure side of her makes me wary. As if she's two different people in one beautiful, supple body.

"I know you can, Vixen." I lift her in my arms and carry her back to bed. If I'm going undercover, I might as well enjoy the perks.

the past

Tia

His body always molds to mine. We're one. Fixed as an entity. As soon as we're connected, all my demons slink back into the dark. Vivid images of living a life without them tease me, as if it's just out of reach. "Brax," I whimper on his deep thrust into me. My nails claw at him, needing to feel some sort of control. How is it that one man can make me so out of control, yet so powerful at the same time?

"Feel me, Tia." He drives into me again and again. "That's me, *my* fucking dick inside you. I want you," he grunts, over and over again.

Wait, what? His mouth falls to mine, stealing my unspoken question in a heated kiss.

Our tongues duel in an erotic tumble, fighting for dominance, and my body bows toward him. Aching for more. For something rough and hard. Deep and almost violent.

Pulling my mouth away, I beg, I fucking plead for it. "Fuck me, Brax, hard, please!" His gaze darkens, from shimmering gold to a dark, deep caramel, and suddenly he pulls out of me. With one hand on my neck, he pulls me to my feet, fire blazing behind his eyes.

As if a rabid animal has been let out of his cage, he lifts me and walks us toward the door, and now I'm even more confused than I was earlier. His thick, hard cock bounces between his legs as he stops at the cold, concrete wall. "This what you want?" He pins me to it with one strong hand.

"Yes," I manage to croak out.

He doesn't answer, only offering a devilish smirk. With his free hand, he lifts my thigh, hooking it around his waist, and thrusts back into me. So fast, so deep, and so fucking violently I feel as if I've been split in half. I cry out, but he swallows the sound with his mouth. Licking at my lips, he takes the lower one between his teeth and bears down, biting until tears spring to my eyes.

I don't know where this man came from, but he's got me dripping fucking wet. His hold on my throat tightens, and my vision blurs. His cock hits me deep, over and over again, rubbing against my G-spot, and I feel everything tighten below my belly button. Desire, lust, and hunger swirl together in my mind, through my body, and they gather at my core. My clit throbs, and my nipples are pebbled, aching for his mouth. But he doesn't give me what I want. What I need.

Instead, he fucks me. Like a primal need has taken hold, a possession unlike anything I've ever seen. His body glistens with sweat, and his mouth lifts at one side. "Do you like being fucked like this?" he hisses between pearly white teeth.

With every thrust, I'm left breathless.

"You love my cock in your tight little cunt, don't you? So fucking tight, so beautifully wet. Just—" Thrust. "For—" Thrust. "Me." Before I can respond, his fingers dig into my neck, and my vision clouds. I'm about to pass out when he releases me, and instead, reaches for my clit and pinches it harshly, sending me spiraling into an abyss of euphoria.

I cry out, again and again. His name echoes through my bedroom. He doesn't relent; instead, he continues ploughing into me, drawing another orgasm from deep inside me. From my very fucking core. My mouth crashes onto his shoulder, and I bite down hard. My teeth break the surface of his smooth skin, and I taste it. The metallic flavor of Braxton Carter. It courses into my veins like a drug. Every nerve in my body sparks with desire.

Electric currents race through my body, and I shudder violently, as if he's shocked me. I cry out again as his finger dips into the tight ring of muscle of my ass. He pistons unforgivingly in and out of my drenched core. My body pulses, sucking him in, craving him, and needing him. "Come for me, Tia. Make that pussy fucking coat me in your sweet honey," he growls, his mouth on my neck. He bites down on the sensitive skin there, sending my world spiraling, and all that's left is us.

And then black.

"You're beautiful when you're sleeping, Vixen." A deep rumble, heavy with sleep, comes from behind me, but I don't open my eyes. I want to savor this feeling of happiness and contentment just a moment longer. I know as soon as I open my eyes, I'll be bombarded with questions.

"I've told you watching me while I sleep is

creepy," I murmur sleepily.

"You love it when I'm creepy." He leans in close, his naked torso hot against my bare back. "You love it even more when I fuck you deep and hard, when I hurt you with my cock. Don't you, baby?" Mention of him taking me has my body pulsing and reacting. I'm so needy for him.

"Don't tease, Braxton." I smile, still not looking at him. The sheet that was covering me moves, and I'm left naked to his heated stare. I feel it as if he's stroking me with his fingertips. Soft, cooling breath teases my skin, from my shoulder down my arm. When he reaches my hip, I whimper, and I know he's smirking. His hot breath trails over the fevered flesh of my thighs all the way to my ankles.

"On your back, Vixen," he demands, and I obey. I can't deny him anything. My thighs splay, my body seems to liquefy under his lust-filled eyes. They darken to a thick caramel, glowing with hunger as he drinks in every inch of me. He reaches out, stroking my thighs, his thumbs massaging the sensitive skin as he nears my sex. "So fucking beautiful. You're always wet for me. Aren't you, baby?" Biting my lip, I moan while nodding as his one calloused thumb skims my bare lips.

A growl, low and feral, breaks from deep in his throat. My eyes meet his before he dives between my legs and sucks my clit into his mouth so hard I yelp at the sensation. So harsh it has me clawing at his scalp. Pulling and tugging his hair as he devours me.

His mouth latched onto my center is enough to have my hips bucking into his face, needing more. He knows what I like. He plays my body like he plays with my heart, an instrument he uses to coerce the most erotic symphony, which echoes around us, filling my room with lust and sex.

"Please, please, oh, God, *please* . . ." My moans get louder and louder. Braxton's mouth taunts and teases, attempting to draw my orgasm directly from my goddamned soul.

"Mmm," he hums against my clit before biting down and driving two fingers into my pussy, making my body convulse. Crooking two fingers, he presses against that special spot, which sends me spiraling on the crest of waves crashing through me, causing my release to soak him. "So fucking delicious." He laps at me, licking and laving at every drop I have to offer.

"Oh, God . . ."

"Now I feel like fucking you. On your knees,

Vixen." He sits back, a thick, proud erection jutting obscenely at me. Gripping my hips, he flips me onto my stomach, and I shuffle onto my knees. My body opens for him, inviting him to do to me what he pleases.

Two big hands grip the globes of my ass, and his hot breath whispers over my puckered entrance. My body tingles in anticipation, and his thumb teases the ring of muscle. "So pretty and tight," he groans.

I glance back to watch him lick me from my clit to my ass. "Please, just fuck me," I beg, louder, needier. Wanting him.

He spits on the tight hole, teasing a finger inside me while flicking my clit with his other hand. His taunting ministrations send me climbing higher and higher. Scissoring two fingers into me, he prepares me for his cock. I'm about to find my release when he stops. Before I can beg, the slick tip of his shaft teases my ass.

"Ready for me, Vixen?"

"Yessss!" I hiss out as he slowly penetrates me. Two fingers plunge into my drenched core, and his cock fills my ass. Deeper, hard, and faster. He pulls out, then thrusts back in.

"You feel me, Tia? You are mine. Remember that," he commands with a gravely tone, fucking my ass, fingering my pussy. Owning me. Because he does. I fist the sheet. His free hand grips my hair, tugging me toward him, arching my back. "Do you like this, baby? Mmm? Me owning both your fucking holes?" He grunts, and my body tightens, needing my release. Aching for my orgasm.

"Please, please, I need to come," I beg again.

"Come, Vixen, on my cock and fingers. Now," he commands, and I obey. My body complies, my heart fills, and my mind lets go of all the horror.

The only thing that exists is the two of us, and I see stars.

Moments later, Braxton joins me. In heaven. In hell. In euphoria.

the present
Tia

"Hello, Tia." She smiles at me. She always seems so happy. "I'm glad you came today. I thought you'd evade me after the last session."

Shaking my head, I flop into my usual seat. Her office is dark today. The clouds outside are dreary, casting everything in a gray haze. Kind of like my mind.

"I need answers. I need to know what the fuck is wrong with me." Another wince. Surely by now she's used to my cursing.

"Well, it's not that easy or straightforward. I've never had a patient with your . . ." She glances at her notepad, then lifts her eyes to meet mine with a sadness etched on her perfect, flawless skin. "It's new to me. To be honest, it's baffled me since the hypnotherapy session when you went away. It's as if you walked out into another room, and I couldn't find you."

She's talking, but I don't understand.

"You've got two varied issues, Tia," she mumbles softly. Almost as if she's scared to tell me. My heart thuds.

Thud. Thud. Thud.

"I'm sick? Very sick?"

She smiles sadly and shakes her head, but shrugs. What. The. Fuck? "Tia, I want you to keep an open mind. This is something I've not yet dealt with. So, as we go through what I've found out, I need you to keep calm."

Sitting back, I pull my legs up and under me, watching her intently, waiting for the bomb to drop. I can't be doing this. How the hell am I meant to exact revenge on my father when I'm sick? When I'm crazy?

"Tia, look at me." Her voice lowers, and I drag my gaze to hers. "You've created a place to go when you're scared, or when things get to be too much. I'd call it an imaginary world, a place of safety in your mind. It's not uncommon. The technical term is paracosm. I've never treated anyone who's done this, so I'm intrigued."

"What do you mean? What about her? The . . . I don't know, woman? She talks to me. Is that even real? Fuck this." She winces again, and I want to laugh. To giggle like a giddy schoolgirl who's angered her mother by cursing.

"Simply put, it's a detailed, imaginary world. They would originate in childhood, if said child has been through a tragedy, or suffered a death of a loved one. It's a way the child copes with the trauma. You're not ill. It's seen as a highly intelligent way of coping. However—"

"Wait. You're telling me I'm living in an imaginary world?" My incredulous tone leaves her gaping. She's got to be kidding. I'm living in a nightmare, and she's telling me I'm making shit up.

"Look, Tia, this is an incredible way of coping. These paracosms are important in you continuing a life and allowing you to orientate yourself in the real world, in real life. Now, you mentioned a girl . . ." She tapers off, meeting my glare.

"I'm not here for you to tell me I'm a child making up shit, doctor. I'm here for you to fix me. I need your expertise to mend the broken parts of my brain." My tone drops to a hoarse whisper, filled with emotion.

"There's one more avenue I'd like to talk about. But before we do, I need to get into that mind of yours. I want you to open up to me. I want to talk to her."

Shaking my head swiftly, I push off the chair and pace the length of her office back and forth. "I can't. There's no way I can bring her here. She does things. Things I can't allow myself to show you."

"Like what, Tia? Does she tell you to do things to others?" Her question startles me, and I freeze. She knows. There's no doubt she knows, and she's not helping me.

I need air.

She wants to talk to me.

No. No. You can't.

Why not?

You're not meant to be here. This is mine. My life.

It's ours. We're in this together.

"No, you have to go."

"Who, Tia?" I glance into deep brown eyes, and she waits. She always waits.

"Nobody. I have to go. I have a meeting with Braxton."

"Have you told him?" she asks. She always asks.

"No, I can't tell him. He can't know how fucked up I am. I'll lose him." I've never been scared of losing someone. My feelings have never been an issue for me. But Braxton seems to have cracked my shell. As scary as that is, I want him. He's burrowed himself inside me, and I have no way of getting him out.

"Why on earth do you think he'll leave you?" She sounds so confused, more so than I feel most days. And to be honest, I'm not sure how to answer her. I'm not perfect by any means. He's someone who needs a woman who can give him everything. How can I do that?

"I don't know." It's the most honest answer I can offer.

A small smile on her lips tells me I'm in for it now. "He won't leave you. He needs to know your feelings are the same as his."

"How would you know he feels the same?"

"Because I can see it in your eyes." Even though I'm not sure what she means, I shrug it off. "The love he's already given you so far is clearly written all over you. You're glowing, happy, not the broken girl who walked in here months ago."

Perhaps she's right. Maybe, just maybe, I can find happiness.

the past
isabelle

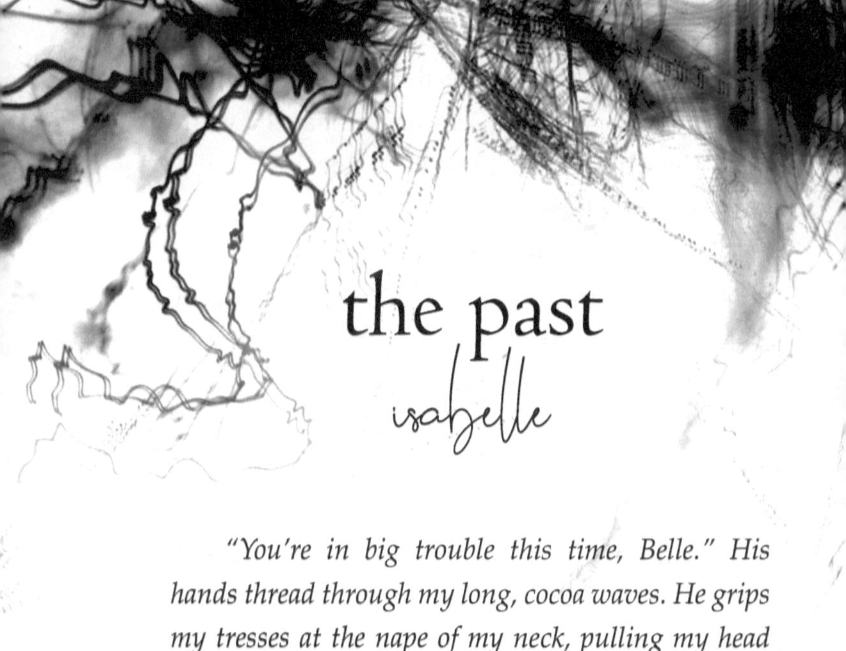

"You're in big trouble this time, Belle." His hands thread through my long, cocoa waves. He grips my tresses at the nape of my neck, pulling my head back, meeting my fearful eyes. "You're all grown up now, aren't you, sweetheart?" His question is dark, dangerous, and fear that was never present when I was around him now threatens to choke me.

As if he can read my mind, he tips his head to the side, regarding me with a malicious glare.

"Father, please, I didn't do it," I whimper, but it's not enough. The kids at school teased me about my family, about the fucked up things my dad did. They all knew about his dealings. So today, when that little asshole called my father a pervert, I freaked out. The teachers had to call him. Now he's angry, and there's nothing I can do to calm him down.

"So, you didn't hit your classmate with a steel

ruler?" I can't deny it because I saw the blood. My hands were ruby red when I woke up. My skirt, shirt, and socks were marred with the crimson liquid. The thick stench of metal permeates around me. Even though I washed my hands, the smell lingers on my clothes. I blacked out and somehow awoke to a flurry of nurses, teachers, and children all glaring at me like I was the antichrist.

"I . . . I didn't mean . . ."

"You never fucking mean to, Belle!" Spittle flies from his mouth as he shouts down at me. "You've caused more trouble since your mother died. Even then, you stood there like a lost sheep. I had to have my men fix your mess. Don't you remember how you ripped her apart? All her blood dripping from your hands? And then, what did you say? It wasn't me. You fuck up all the time!" His body vibrates with rage.

Since they found me standing over my mother's body with her blood all over me, I locked myself away, inside my mind. I found a friend inside my world where it's beautiful and sunny and there's never any pain.

He pushes me away, and I stumble onto the floor. He brought me straight to my bedroom when we arrived home from school, and I thought he was going to lock me inside, but when he entered with me,

I was shocked. He hardly ever comes inside here. I'm sixteen. I'm old enough that if he so much as tries anything, I'll cut him.

Like I taught you.

Yes, like you taught me.

"Get up. Clean yourself up. You look like shit," *he growls, but I don't move fast enough, and with a swift kick to my stomach, the wind gets knocked from me.* "I said get the fuck up!" *Quicker this time, I push off the carpet and scramble for the door.*

Once inside my bathroom, I shut myself away, locking him out. My ribs protest, and the agony shoots through me.

"And when you're done, get yourself out here. I've got some friends coming over." *With that, I hear my bedroom door shut and lock.*

Imprisoned.

Break out. Kill him.

I can't, he's my father.

And? He's an asshole, Bella girl.

"I know, but right now, I need to finish school and then I can leave," *I whisper, and I feel the ebb and flow of her leaving me to my tasks at hand.*

Opening the taps, I wait for the water to heat and strip out of my dirty clothes. Once the steam billows around me, I step inside. My ribs protest, and I try inhaling a deep, calming breath. Relaxing, however, never comes.

Moments later, I hear the music start. Men's deep voices filter through the doors, and I realize the party must have started. Back in my bedroom, I dress quickly, pulling on a pair of faded black jeans over a pair of cotton panties, a long-sleeved sweater over a dark blue tank top, and my socks.

I'm about to pull on my sneakers when my bedroom door flies open. My father is dressed in khakis and a gray T-shirt, and he stalks over to me. "What are you wearing? That won't work. Where's your pretty pink dress? The one you wore to the school dance?"

"But I can't wear that dress tonight." My mouth falls open on a gasp. The dress in question is skintight, and it stops just above my knee. It's a formal dance dress. There's no way I'm wearing it in front of I-don't-know-how-many men.

"You can and you will. Change. Now." I wait for him to leave, but when he doesn't, I push off the bed and head into my walk-in closet and pull out the cerise material, which matches the deep pink ballet flats. "Do it in here," he orders in a gruff tone, and I gasp in shock. "Now."

In my bedroom, I find him seated on my bed, his arms crossed over a broad chest. "Could you at least give me some privacy?" My question earns me a glare

I'd rather not see, so I bite my tongue and pull off the sweater. When I reach for my tank top and pull it up over my head, I meet his intense stare as soon as the material falls to the floor.

My breasts are bare to his gaze, and unease slowly sweeps over me. I reach for my bra, but he stretches out, gripping my wrist. "Leave it." I open my mouth to retort, but bite back the comment, knowing it would earn me more than just a swift kick in the ribs.

He releases my hand, and I reach for my dress before pulling it over my head and shimmy it down my body. I then unbutton my jeans and shove them off.

"Good girl. Now take your panties off and meet me downstairs. If you try anything funny, I'll make you fucking regret it." I'm left alone to make the final change he requested, and the fear I felt earlier returns with a vengeance.

Tonight, isn't a party. Tonight, I'm being auctioned.

My head spins from the memory. I remember the night perfectly, as if it was yesterday. The pain and sadness were enough to send me spiraling. To take the slow lick of dread and mark me forever. My father sold me, and I was sent into hell. He smiled and waved me off as I walked out of the house I called home for sixteen years.

Everything that happened to me that night and all the nights after changed me.

I've become this.

I had no choice.

I chose this life.

The life of a murderer.

They'll find you.

They know where you are.

I may have killed my captors, but I haven't killed the one who sold me. Pulling on my leather shorts, I zip them up and pivot in front of the mirror. My ass is curvy, sexy, and I know it's the one way I'll get into the compound. I inherited my long, dark curls from my mother. Having an African American mother and a Spanish father has given me beauty beyond my imagination. My tanned skin and dark eyes make for an alluring vision. That's what they used to sell me.

My curves are hugged by leather and lace. Tonight, the club is my first stop, then on to the warehouse. Grabbing the sleek, silver blade, I slide it into my knee-high, onyx suede boots. One last look at my makeup, and I head into my living room, grab my purse and keys, and then make my way down to the car.

I've been driving my jet-black Benz for

three years, and the darkened windows give me privacy as well as hide the gun that always rests on the passenger seat when I'm alone.

I wonder if he'll be at the club tonight.

A man like no other. Sexy, handsome, and strong. Those honey-colored eyes pierce everyone he stares at. There's an awareness to him, something different, as if he's searching for something, or someone.

The first time I saw him, I wanted him. Scrap that, I fucking *needed* him. But when I saw him leave with *her*, I knew I didn't have a chance. Not for long though. I'll weave my way into his life. One way or another. I've been doing this too long to lose to that bitch.

He'll be mine. Her life will be mine.

She plays the sweet, innocent act too well, but the thing is, she doesn't know I'm back. She thinks she's safe, but she's so far from it. She'll never be safe again. Not until I finish what was started all those years ago. Not until her final breath. The last one she'll take, and I know that, because I'll be the one to deliver the final blow.

the past
braxton

"This is it." I stab at the screen. Grant stares at the information, but all I get is a deep grunt. Ignoring him, I continue. Renewed confidence has my mind spinning at what I can do. "We can take this asshole down. I'll find that fucker and make him pay. Miguel Alvarez will beg for his life, and I'll show no mercy." Even though the search ends here, I'll keep digging. I'll dig so fucking deep until there's a hole big enough for her father to fit into.

"And you're going to do this with my help," he states matter-of-factly, giving me a no nonsense look I can't refuse.

"Thanks, man. This is almost ten years in the making, just to find out that the girl I'm fucking is related to that monster."

"You mean the girl you're falling for?" he

challenges. Snapping my gaze to his, I open my mouth to respond, but shut it again, because deep down, I know he's right. There's no doubt I'm falling for Tia. "It's written all over your face, man, no need to deny it. I'm sure everyone's noticed, including her."

"If she has, she hasn't said anything. I didn't give her a chance." My mind flits back to last night when she found me in the living room drinking her bourbon. I didn't tell her I'd found her purse or discovered her real name, and I should've. I promised her I'd wait, but I'm not sitting around. She's going to have to trust me.

Somehow, I doubt she knows about her father's dealings, and if she does, it puts her in more danger than we thought. There's something else about her, something she's hiding, and I'll find out what it is.

Grant slumps into the chair beside my desk and watches me. "What?" I ask without meeting his intense gaze. "Spit it out, man."

"This girl, I know she's something special to you. I'm not telling you how to live your life, because fuck knows I don't even know how to live mine, but just be honest with her. Tell her about your folks, what happened to them, who killed them. Allow her to understand. And I think you should tell her about your search for her father. If you're serious about her, and she about you, then nothing can come between that."

I stare open-mouthed at him. I've known this man for so long, and we've never really spoken openly about our personal lives. It's always been work, but as I look at him, I can see there's a man behind the soldier exterior. "I'll think about it. Right now, she's not giving me her full story, so I don't want to freak her out and have her running for the hills. I want her with me all the way." My confession startles us both, because his eyes widen in shock. My expression must give away the same emotion because he smirks then, nodding in understanding. Never in my life did I think I'd fall so deeply, but I am. I've done it.

Deep down, I wonder if Mom and Dad would have been proud of me. Of her. If I brought her home, I know my mother would have fussed over her. I just wonder if she is my forever, or am I barking up the wrong tree?

She's got a lot she's hiding. I'm curious to see how this plays out. If we'll move past this hurdle and both learn to trust. Finding out that her father is the owner of the club we're taking down is a breakthrough. I'd love to walk in there right now and fuck his shit up, take down the sick fuck once and for all, but I know we've got to do this right.

With rules to follow, I need to calm down and go into it with a rational head. Although, who am I kidding? I'm never rational around her. She's like a fucking storm, sweeping through my life, and taking down everything in her wake. And I'm gladly letting her do it.

I didn't think about falling for her all those times I sat in the bar and watched her flirt with my best friend, but since he's out of the picture, and I've gotten to know her, I can safely say she was made for me. All she needs to do is let me into that stubborn head of hers.

It's one of those days, the heat is unbearable, and I'm pulling on my white sleeveless tank when I hear the call come through. "Hey, man, we need to get out of here now." I glance at my partner, Ryker. He's been my best friend since we were kids. When I signed up, so did he.

"Let's jet." I grab my belt, looping it through my uniform pants, and we head out into the blistering heat. Our regiment has been deployed here for three

years. We've not been on the frontline, but we've seen some pretty gruesome shit.

Jumping into the Jeep, Ryk starts the engine, and we tear out of the compound into the main city. Everything is brown. Dust settles on every surface, and if I closed my eyes, I would be able to tell exactly what everything looks like still. This tiny town we've overtaken has become home. Each house looks the same, but the people, they're the ones who are different.

It's painful, heart-wrenching to see the hurt in their eyes. They live with the threat of murder, death, and losing limbs on a daily basis. It's sickening that we're here to defend them when it's their own people trying to hurt them. "Watch! Watch!" Pivoting, I glance at the teenage boy screaming at us. Before I have time to react, something lifts the jeep, flinging me from the seat.

There's screaming, the heat burns, and suddenly, there's black.

Shaking my head of the memory, I check the time and realize I've got to get going. I'm meant to be meeting my girl in twenty minutes. I haven't heard from her all day. Granted, we've been busy at HQ setting up our plan to take down the fucker, Miguel Alvarez, and his fucked up club.

The dangers involved mean we have to take every precaution. We can't lose men on this job, and I'm concerned about Ryker. He's been AWOL for almost a week. When he stormed out of the office, he didn't come back, and he hasn't responded to calls or messages.

He's a grown-ass man, but deep down, I know he's also a broken kid. His life hadn't been easy. Losing his mother at an early age left him with a man who was an alcoholic. Most of his childhood was spent at my house, and as we grew up together, I saw the bruises and scars on his arms and legs.

Now when I look back on it, I should have told someone. I just hope he can get his life back together.

Pushing off the chair, I grab my jacket and shrug it on. With my phone in hand, I send a quick message to Tia letting her know I'm on my way. As I head down the stairs, Grant glances up and crooks his finger, calling me over.

"You should see this man." He points to the screen. When I lean in, I notice a woman, beautiful, with long, dark hair walking alongside Ryk. They're heading into Innuendo. What the hell is he playing at?

I can't see the woman's face, but from her profile, she looks like Tia. "He's going to the club we're going to raid in two days?"

"Looks like he's with your girl," Grant remarks quietly. He's right; she looks very much like my woman, but it can't be. *Can it?*

Pulling my phone from my pocket, I hit dial on her number. It rings and rings but ends up going to voicemail. This doesn't make sense. She hates him. *Why would she be going out with him?*

My mind races with confusion, and my heart hammers in my chest. I should go there. Find the man I used to call *best friend* and knock him the fuck out. Jealousy abates, leaving anger in its place.

"I'm coming with you," Grant says quickly. I glance at the man beside me as he rises and grabs his holster and jacket. "Let's go."

Without a word, we head out to my car, and when I peel out of the parking lot, the only thing on my mind is how the fuck I'm going to stay calm and not kill Ryker.

"Shit!" Grant's growl drags my attention from the road. "Pull over, now!" he orders gruffly, and I do. Luckily, we're on a quiet road. When I put the car in park, he hands me his phone.

I read the email from our intel guy, and my

blood runs cold. Words blur, my mind races, and my heart thuds painfully against my rib cage. Tia's medical records. *FUCK!*

the present

Tia

"So, you're in love?" she asks me in her quiet way. The word love is a foreign concept. I haven't felt it for so long. I've become accustomed to anger, hatred, and sadness. Perhaps love is something people only claim to feel. "Tia, do you love Braxton? You can tell me. Anything you're feeling, you need to embrace."

I nod.

"And does he love you too?" A small smile plays on her lips at the question, which makes me grin. He does love me. I know he does. Even though we've not said those words to each other, I know he loves me. I see it in his eyes. Those caramel pools shine like gold when he looks at me.

Perfect.

"Tia, you'll need to tell him the truth soon.

You can't live a lie with him. If you love each other, there's only one thing you need to do, and that's come clean. Don't you want to be clean, Tia?" Her question jolts me out of the reverie of happiness and dips me into the dark, inky blackness.

"You know I can't tell him. If I do, he'll leave. Just like everyone good in my life."

"Lies are not the way to build a relationship, Tia. There are things you'll need to tell him before you can form a bond. And from the look in your eyes, you've already fallen deeply in love with him." She's right as she always is. She's inside my mind, reading it like an open book. Am I an open book? Are my pages bared for all to see?

"Lies are the only thing I have to hold on to. They're a constant," I tell her harshly. It's rude. My anger rises like a slow, licking fire, heating my blood that rushes through every vein in my body.

"Sometimes you have to let go of your past," she murmurs, scribbling on her notebook. As if she's writing letters to someone. *To my father? To me?*

"Letting go means walking away from my goal. My plan. Everything I've worked so hard for. If he knows, if he ever learns who I am, I'm not sure I'll be free. He'll have me locked up, and they'll throw away the fucking key."

She nods. Agreement swirls in the air around us, and I know she's contemplating how to go ahead with this. How does she expect me to walk away from Braxton?

If he knows about my sordid past, it will be the end of something before it ever started. I've never wanted more, never wanted someone to love me. But with him, I do.

"I love him. I'm not losing him because you told me to," I bite out harshly. "This is my life, not yours. Have you ever loved someone more than your own life and didn't understand why? Did you ever feel so complete with someone that the moment they step out the door you're once again a fragment of what they make you? And tell me something, have you ever looked into someone's eyes and truly known that you were made for them? That the reason you were born was to be their partner, their wife, or husband, that they make you whole?"

My tirade stops as she regards me with an expression akin to pity. Sadness mars her face. Soft, smooth skin crinkles into a frown, her dark brows knit together, and her eyes darken with fear, anger, and frustration.

It's been so long, and she's no closer to figuring me out than I am to finding out why I'm here. *Why do I come here every week?* I don't know.

It's not like it's helping me. My mind is still fucking broken. The only thing right in my life is the man I love. "This is over. This will be the last time I come here." I stalk past her and head toward the door.

"Tia," she calls quietly, and when I turn, her eyes glisten with unshed tears. "Come back. Just give me one more day." Her plea is heartfelt. So much emotion. So much love. Confusion settles in my mind once again, but I don't give her an answer. I twist the door handle and step through the threshold into normality.

the past
isabelle

"You think I wanted this? My life was never as perfect as yours!" My voice is shrill in the dark. Her pretty face is still so perfect, even after I slapped her, even after I punched her. Hate spirals through me like a venomous serpent slithering, ready to strike.

"I don't know what you're talking about." A melodic voice filled with fear, anger, and rage is music to my ears. Everything about her being tied up at my mercy shoots adrenaline through me.

She's always been the innocent one.

The favorite.

Not anymore. She's going to pay, slowly, filled with the pain I had to live through. She'll experience every inch of her skin aching, bleeding, and burning. Her body and mind will join mine in the darkest depths.

"Please, don't hurt me. I don't know who you are." Her pleas turn me on. Yes, they do. So fucking hot. Every time I begged and pleaded, they would only fuck me harder, deeper, rougher. Until I couldn't walk. Shaking my head of the memory, I grab the scalpel. Her eyes are still covered with a thick, black blindfold, and I know her hearing will be prickling from the sound.

Using their methods, the same ones they used on me, I know how it feels, I know how it sounds. As I near her, I see the tremble that shakes her. Fear. So, fucking beautiful.

When I found Ryker, saw him with her, I knew he could be swayed. I watched him for months. Saw how he would fuck every woman from here to the East Coast. The moment I stepped up and flirted with him, he bit the poisoned apple I held out, and he was mine.

It didn't take long for me to whisper dark thoughts to him. He admitted he was only with her to pass the time. But then he learned about my past, about how she didn't do anything to help me survive the pain and agony I had been put through. I made sure he heard every sordid detail. The darkness inside him came to life, I saw it flourish. And I made him feel for me what I knew he couldn't feel for her. Yes, I may have painted her as the bad sister, but that's only because it's true.

She spent her life as the apple of daddy's eye while I was sold off into the trade where I learned more about torture than I care to admit. But now it's come in handy because I have knowledge she could never fathom. Having Ryker turn on her will ensure she sees how weak she really is. Thinking she could use him; she will learn that she's nothing more than a broken toy.

For a long time, I thought I was the shattered one, but her mind broke long before mine ever did. I'm strong. I was meant to lead, and I'll have everything she could never dream of because I've survived.

Ryker's promise to stand by me as I finish this off has given me renewed strength. And seeing her pain as she realizes he was only with her because I pushed him toward her will make this revenge that much sweeter.

I smile because I knew all along, he was the man for me.

"You do know who I am. Or did you block that out as well?" I whisper quietly. I know she recognizes me. Her head shakes left to right again. Gripping the hair at the nape of her neck, I tug back, my mouth at her ear. "You will learn what happens to little princesses. My life has been a nightmare. My nightmares haunt me, and you know why? Because your precious little face was too fucking innocent."

"What? I don't understand. Let me go!" If I pleaded like this with them, I'd have been whipped and beaten. She should be grateful I'm not them.

"I don't think so, Tia. You need to pay—"

"Any amount. I have money. Please, just—"

"Shut up! You're not paying in cash. You're paying with blood," I hiss in her ear. Another shudder of fear wracks her body, and she cries out when I slide the metal down the side of her cheek. A prickle of red leaks from her tanned skin.

A tiny slit, but the trickle of blood is so pretty. So perfect. "Why are you doing this?" Her questions are grating on my nerves, scraping and clawing against me. I take a step back and grab the cloth lying on the table and stuff it in her mouth. Muffled cries now echo in the expansive space. It's almost sunset, but the deep orange of the sun's rays shines through the dark blinds on the one window to my right. This was the only place I could bring her without getting noticed. This abandoned warehouse which is an enormous building on the wrong side of the tracks. Nobody will find her here, since no one knows my father owns them. His name isn't on the deeds.

It's cooling as the sun settles on the horizon. The apartment itself is bare besides the small sofa and cardboard boxes against the wall—with no heating. Her body shivers, and I know it's a mix of fear and cold.

The sounds of steps near me catch my attention, and when I glance up, I see my man. The one who helped me.

"Is our guest comfortable?" he asks.

When she stills, I know she's recognized his voice, but she can't say anything, thankfully.

"She is, for now," I inform him with a smirk.

He reaches out and strokes her cheek lightly, and she flinches away.

"Hello, Tia," he murmurs against her ear. "You look lovely all tied up. You didn't tell me you enjoyed it, or I would have done it to you instead of your sister every time I needed release."

Jealousy, unbidden, flares to life, shooting through me. Why is it always her? What is so fucking special about *her*? "Are you going to stand there all day and taunt her?" Dark eyes pierce me when he places a hand on my throat.

"Do you want me to fuck you? Do you want her to watch us?" Images of what he's asking flit through my mind like a dirty movie. My mind is fucked up. Everything I've endured makes me want that. I want someone to be rough, to tie me up, and to hurt me. I get off on that shit, and so does he. So I nod.

He reaches over and snatches the blindfold off her face. Eyes bulge when she looks between us. Those pretty blue eyes glare at him, but it's when her gaze settles on me, that's when recognition appears. It's a slow burning flame which teases just behind those baby blues.

Lifting one side of my mouth, I glare at her as the smirk forms in slow motion on my face. The hand gripping my neck tightens, seizing my attention from the woman I spent my life in competition with. Even when I was held captive, there was nothing but her. They spoke of her all the time. Told me how much prettier she was, how she would have made them more money.

"Hello, Tia," I murmur again, meeting her angry, shocked glare. "How are you, little sister?"

"Enough family fun." A deep rumble comes

from the man who has me in a chokehold. "Let's play." He drags me over to the sofa, and I feel her eyes on me. Burning me. Boring into me like a drill bit, inch by motherfucking inch.

He reaches for my tank top and tugs it off, so rough it tears down the front. My bare breasts are at his mercy as he lunges forward, taking a pebbled bud into his mouth. My fingers rake through his unruly chocolate curls as I hold him to my chest.

Glancing over, I watch my little sister pierce me with intensity unlike anything ever. His mouth moves to the other nipple, suckling and biting down enough to earn him my whimpers. Already, his hands are fumbling with my jeans. A hiss of the zipper and the whoosh of them traveling down my slim legs are the only sounds around us besides him sucking on my flesh.

Muffled pleas fall on deaf ears as his deft fingers find my clit, circling it. He teases his digits into my core, pumping in and out at a mind-altering pace. It's so slow, and all I want is a fast and furious fuck.

When he finally unlatches his mouth from my breasts, he glances at her, at the woman who shares my bloodline, and smirks. "Your sister tastes so much better than you ever did, Tia."

An evil grin curls on his lips as he spins me around, bending me over the arm of the sofa. We both have an incredible view of her face, tears streaming down her cheeks.

In one swift move, his cock impales me. Fully seated, he stills for a moment. "And her cunt is so tight around me. I'm so glad I didn't waste my time on you." He pulls out and drives back in, harder, rougher, and when he tugs my hair, pulling me up against his chest, he hisses in my ear, "You're mine, aren't you, Belle?"

I can't help mewling my answer. "Yes, I'm all yours, Ryker."

the past

Tia

Memories of what happened flit through my thoughts.

Ryker in my apartment, wanting to talk.

I poured a drink, he finished his beer, and mine . . .

I don't remember. Why can't I remember?

He drugged me. He must have.

And now I'm here.

My mind races, as if there's something twirling inside it. My psychologist told me this would happen because of what I witnessed as a child. I retreated to a safe place in order to cope with the trauma. She explained my mind isn't right. It doesn't work like others.

Paracosm.

One word that means nothing to others, but means everything to me. My heart thuds. My body tenses. It hurts. Everything hurts. Only Braxton made it okay. Only he fixed me. Now, I'm here, thrown back into the world I escaped.

My father told me I was broken. He couldn't auction me to others; he had to deal with me. That's when it first happened. When it all went to shit.

I found out what happened that day. The day my mother drowned in a pool of blood. My mind was locked away. Hidden in the world I created. There, I was safe. It was only there that I was a normal little girl. Where she was. My friend, my enemy, the other half of who I am.

You see, my father, Miguel Alvarez, is a monster, and I vowed to kill him.

But this . . . this doesn't make sense. Belle is my sister. How can she want to hurt me? What did I do? Dad told me she had to go away for school. And, of course, I believed the lies. But what could have happened to her to make her act like this?

It's dark inside my world, my mind. She's not here.

Where are you?

I'm here. Now that Mr. Perfect isn't here, you need me?

Please, I need to get out of here.

You've fucked it, Tia. This is how you die. How we die.

No, you have to help me.

I can't. Not this time.

My eyes meet Ryker's, the man who was in my bed, but thankfully, never in my body, or my heart. I never loved him, but for a moment I cared. *Isn't that enough?* I'm watching my sister get fucked by my ex-boyfriend. "You see this, Tia? He wants me. Not you." Her words slice me. Not that I want Ryk, but the venom she spits them with pains me. Nothing but hatred coats her tone, and I can't imagine what I could have done to make her have so much anger and animosity toward me.

It's all your fault.

You're the perfect one.

You're the one they choose.

The taunting starts, and my head aches, throbbing painfully, dragging me into the darkness of my mind. My medication. She doesn't know I need my pills. My eyes flutter closed; my mind flits to Brax. I wonder if he knows I'm gone. Does he even realize that something's happened to me?

Hands grip my face, and my eyes fly open to find Ryk staring at me. "Didn't like that, did you? Seeing my dick hard for someone else. All the months I was with you, it wasn't real. The worst time of my life, acting like this" — his big, rough hand cups my pussy through the thin yoga pants — "made me want you. Every time I was near you, I pictured her." He points to Belle. "That's why I could never bring myself to fuck you."

My mouth is still gagged by the cloth, and I can't answer him. I can't tell him I hate him. That I'm in love with Braxton. But all my words die on my tongue. Bile rises, filling my mouth with a sour taste, and tears spring to my eyes. He thinks it's because of what he said because the satisfied look on his face tells me so.

He's going to hurt you now.

No, please, don't let him. Take me away. We can go to the candy store. I beg of you, please.

I'm leaving you now, little girl. It's time you grow up and fight your own battles.

Deep-rooted fear hits me when I feel a cold sting on my flesh. A shimmering blade slices down my middle. It doesn't break the skin, only my clothing. A cold rush of air hits my now naked body, and Ryker steps back to regard his work.

"This body of yours will be so fucked up that

your little boyfriend will never want you again. He'll look at you with disgust. Does he even know what you did when you were younger? How you used to fuck all those men? Belle told me about it."

He glances at my sister who's sitting on the sofa, clad in her small leather skirt and Ryker's T-shirt, with a cigarette in her plump lips, billowing white smoke around her, making her look scarier than she did earlier.

I can't respond, and I resign myself to the fact that there's nothing I can do. "Did you like it?" he sneers. "I bet you loved the attention, all those filthy fucker's hands on you," he spits, and my heart aches as the memory steals me.

"Come on, Tia. You're fucking useless to me when you're broken, but you can still make me a few scraps." Dad pulls me down the hallway by my upper arm. It hurts where his fingers dig into my flesh, but I don't cry out. He doesn't like when I do. He hates it. That's when he hits me. Strikes me with his hand or with whatever he can find.

I don't like bruises. I don't like the pain. I don't know what he means, but when he drags me into the living room, I see two of his friends sitting there. I recognize them because Daddy took me to work one day. To the club he owns.

"There she is," the one with a scar running down his cheek says, smirking at me. "Come here, little one, I need to get a good look at you." His smirk is dark, and his leering eyes rake over me, sending revulsion coursing through me.

Before I can answer, Dad pushes me forward, and I stumble toward the man. Fear seeps into my veins, unbidden and painful, like something is burning me from the inside out. When I glance down to where the man has a hold on me, I notice the plastic casing of a syringe. He put something in me.

"She'll calm down once this is in her bloodstream," he says, looking behind me at my dad. Sixteen years, and it's only been him, but now, I'm no longer just his to use. I'll be theirs too. These men are going to take me. The confidence with which I know this, has fear coursing through me.

Hands tug at me, at my clothes. I wish I could close my eyes. I wish my mind didn't know what they were doing, but it does. I can see it happening.

Fight them.

I can't.

They're evil. They need to die.

She always tells me things I know. She tells me the truth.

My eyes are open, and I watch them, but I'm

sitting on my sofa at home. Not my real home. The one in my mind. The place that I'm safe. Where my friend is. She's the only one who loves me. She keeps me safe beside her. Fingers, mouths, hands. They're on my skin. It burns and prickles. "So sweet, aren't you, little one?"

They're talking, but I don't answer.

I can't.

I don't feel. I'm numb.

More fingers. Something bigger. Thicker. Pain. Searing, burning, excruciating.

I can't close my eyes. I can't. Tears stream down my cheeks. Then another white-hot pain hits me from behind. More tears. I can't breathe. They're grunting in my ear. My skin stings from their fingers, their hold on me too tight. Then I'm flailing. I'm just a doll, a lifeless rag doll. My body tumbles, and I'm on the floor.

It's as if I'm watching a horror movie.

I want to scream.

I want to fight.

My body is numb.

My limbs are weak, and they don't listen to me. I tell them to move with my mind. But they're no longer connected to my mind. They don't care. I don't care.

Let go, Tia. They'll only hurt you more.

She knows best. So, I listen to her.
She's my only friend.
We sit back on our sofa and watch.

"You're so fucked in the head, aren't you?" Ryker's hand slaps across my face, leaving it smarting from the smack. But it drags me from the morbid memories. Roughly, he pulls the cloth from my mouth, and my lungs suck in air quickly.

"Please, Ryker, just let me go. I don't know wh—"

"Shut up!" Spittle flies from his mouth. He looks demented. This isn't the man I dated. This isn't the man I spent six months with. He's lost inside himself. I know how that feels; I've lived with it for too long. So long, in fact, sometimes I can't remember who I am.

"Ryk, babe, we need to go. Daddy is going to be angry if we spend more time with her. He'll take care of her." The mention of my father sends fear racing through me.

He's found me.

I told you he'd find you.

Shit.

He's going to hurt us, you.

No, I'll get out. Brax will find me.

How do you know?

He promised he'd always find me.

What if he doesn't get to me in time?

Stop. He has to.

Promises don't count.

Yes, they do. Brax counts.

Stop being so fucking naïve and in love.

Love is stronger.

Love is a lie.

No. It's not.

Did you love your daddy?

Shaking my head, I ignore her question. I can't do this. I can't lose it now. I've come so far. Going back to *that* girl isn't going to get me out of this. I need to think clearly. "Belle, what do you mean? Where's Dad?"

She pins me with a fierce glare. "He's coming soon, Tia. When he does, you'll be sorry you fucked him over. You see, your little boyfriend thinks he's clever, but . . ." She tapers off. Pulling a drag on the smoke, she inhales, and it's as if I can see the smoke racing through her body, from her mouth down into her chest. "He's going to find out why Miguel Alvarez is notorious. You see, Tia, after you ran away, Daddy found me and apologized. He told me you were broken, that I was the special one. I am his favorite."

"I don't understand. What are you talking about? He told me you went away to school." I implore her with my eyes, hoping she'll see reason.

"Don't fucking lie to me!" Her screech has me wincing. "He sold me, Tia," she murmurs and almost looks human as she pushes up from the sofa and stalks toward me. "You were the lucky one. You got all Daddy's love. Me? I got raped, every godforsaken day by men I didn't know. I got abused and slapped around," she continues, and my heart crumbles. Tiny shattered pieces of the love I had falls at my feet. He lied. I knew he lied, but I didn't realize how fucked up it was. My poor sister.

"Belle—"

"Do not say my name, *sister.*" She sneers the last word, and it's heavy with venom. "You stayed with him when I was locked in a cell like an animal. I was beaten every fucking day for four years, until *Ryk* saved me." She purrs his name, raking a blood-red fingernail down his bare chest.

"What?" My gaze darts between them, and a laugh falls from her lips. My world spins off its axis. "Do you not know what Dad did to me after you left? When I turned sixteen, he made me do things, Belle, he . . ." My words are silenced by her deadly stare.

"Do not lie to me. He didn't make you do anything." She leans in, her face inches from mine. "He told me about how you went off the rails. How you went around fucking every dick in sight. Daddy told me you'd try to tell me lies about him. You were the one who told him to send me instead of you." Shaking my head so fast, I feel dizzy. It's a lie. It's all lies. "You even killed Mom, just so she didn't save me. You will pay." My stomach turns at the memory of my mother.

Blood.

Red.

No. No. No.

Breathe, Tia. You didn't kill her.

My regression sessions were supposed to give me answers, but that memory is so deeply buried I've never been able to recall the day my mother was killed.

"Let's go, Ryk, she's not worth it." With that, my sister turns and stalks away, her hand latched on Ryker's as they leave me to hang here in the dark.

"Please!" I cry out, but they ignore me. My mind darkens, and the migraine starts.

No. No. No. Please.

the past
braxton

When we stormed the club, we couldn't find Miguel anywhere, but we did capture one of his men. "Where the hell is she?" I spit in his face, but all I get is a maniacal guffaw. This is fucking ridiculous. How am I meant to find her when we have nothing to go on? It's been forty-eight hours, and I haven't heard from her. She's not at her apartment nor at the bar.

Yes, there are times we go without talking, but this has my hackles rising. Something's off, so vastly off that I found this little dick weed. He had a picture of her in his pocket at the club. Walking into that place was painful enough knowing what's about to go down.

Tia is gone, and I don't know where the fuck she is. We've got people scouring the CCTV footage, but nothing's turned up. The girl Ryk was with couldn't have been Tia. I know deep in my heart that she's out there somewhere, and I'm afraid she's hurt. Or worse. No. I can't think like that.

Grant's hand lands on my shoulder, and he tugs me back. "Let me handle this?" he questions, and I see the determination on his face. He'll get what we need. I nod and take a step back. Turning, I head out of the room and into the hallway of the club. It's closed, empty except for the team I brought in. I've only ever seen the front of the bar, but the back where the offices are situated is stark. Void of any color. Like my fucking life without Tia.

She's the only thing I need. I want her back. "We need to get into the offices, the top floor of the club. It's the only way we can figure out what Ryker was doing there."

Grant's right. The first thing we need to find out is why my former best friend was there with a woman who looks like Tia. "We should—"

"Hey man, check this out," Jason calls from the desk, and I'm beside him in moments. The feed picks up the woman who looks like Tia talking to an older man. When he zooms into the image on the screen, my body turns cold. Ice chills my veins and anger fuels my blood.

The fucker who killed my parents. Tia's father. The girl on the screen smiles at him. Leaning in, they hug, and the realization slaps me in the face and punches me in the gut. She's my girl's sister. She must be. "Run an identity scan. I need to know who she is!" I bark, earning a smug grin from Jason.

"Already done." Jason clicks the mouse, and the image in question fills the screen.

Isabelle Alvarez.

Older sister to Tia, or Tatiana Alvarez.

"Their mother?" He clicks the mouse, pulling up another screen, and there it is.

Monique Jones.

Married to Miguel for twenty years, murdered when Tia was nine and Isabelle was twelve. The murder was never solved.

"We need to find Isabelle. She'll be our key to finding Tia, and their father. I need this to end. This fucker needs to meet his maker, and it's happening tonight. I'm not waiting anymore," I bite out to the men in the room. Agreement comes from each of them. They know what this asshole has done, and it's time he pays for his sins. In blood.

"Guys, I've just found his hideout on the outskirts of town. I've also cross-referenced the vehicle registration we've been tracking, and he goes to this place here every night." Jason once again points to the screen at the warehouse which is on the other side of town.

"We'll move out at nightfall. It will be easier to get onto the property undetected. Pull up the blueprints. We need to figure out a point of entry." Our computer whizz nods and starts furiously typing away at the keyboard.

Turning from the guys, I head into the kitchen and grab the coffee pot. My phone buzzing startles me, and I pull it from my pocket to see Ryker's name staring back at me. Swiping my finger over the screen, I grunt my greeting. "What do you want?"

"That's no way to talk to your best friend, Brax. It seems that whore you've been fucking has gotten to you." His tone is thick with malice, and I'm ready to take the fucker down. All those years of friendship growing up together—practically as brothers—is gone.

I'm done. He's had chance after chance, and I've run out of patience. "If you so much as harm a hair on her head, I will bury you. Do you understand me, Ryker?" I slam my fist against the counter so hard everything rattles.

"Jesus, bro, that bitch doesn't have a magic

pussy." He chuckles again, and I'm ready to ram him into a fucking wall. "Not that I would know because I've never been there or done that. Maybe I am missing out on something." He chuckles darkly, and rage courses through my veins.

"Two things. First, I am not your *bro*. Second, if you ever come near her, speak ill of her, or try to hurt her, I will fuck you up so badly you'll be six feet under. And I'm not fucking around. I will kill you, Ryk." My words are harsh, serious, and venomous.

"Oh, it's not me you should be worried about, bro. I'm definitely not going to hurt her. But if her father arrives, which he will be in" — he's quiet for a moment, and I picture him looking at the Rolex he always wears — "about two hours, I doubt you'll find her in time. You see, her father has a grudge. And it doesn't matter if she's his daughter or not, you know what he does to people who cross him."

With that, the line goes dead, and I'm left gawking at the phone. Racing back into the tech room, I find the men scouring pages and pages of plans.

"I just got a call from Ryker. He's just confessed that Tia's father is out to hurt her.

There were sounds in the background, sounded like a train track, possibly a warehouse. Can you pull up all security footage from the warehouses closest to the railway, Jason?"

"We'll find her, man," Grant promises.

I glance at my partner and nod. I know we'll find her. The only question is, in what condition?

✾

"Yes!" My roar is loud and echoes around us. Everyone's eyes are on me. After two hours of searching through security footage, six men, six screens, I find what I'm looking for. The fucker is about an hour from here. My team surrounds me as I hit print on the info I found.

"It's an hour away," Grant says loudly. "If we leave now, we'll be there by nightfall. Let's take this fucker out. I want to shred him."

I glance back at the man behind me and regard the malicious grin that quirks his mouth. Grant is known for his love of knives. And I have a feeling he's ready to exact some revenge, but I can't let him.

Miguel Alvarez is mine.

"This mark is mine. He killed my parents. It's time for me to gut him like he did them. I want to hear him scream, beg, and plead for his life. I want to see the life drain from his eyes. For them. For me. And for Tia." A heavy hand falls on my shoulder, and I regard him.

"Then you'll get it. Let's go." He grabs his jacket and gun belt, which has sheaths for two butcher knives, and he shrugs both on. My holster is all I need, but in case we find Tia and she's hurt, I grab my own jacket, and we race out to the SUV.

The darkened windows allow us anonymity, and I slip into the passenger seat. With Jason taking out the surveillance around the warehouse, I know they won't see us coming, but I'll see them. Him.

Two other vans behind us start up, and the engines roar in the dark night. The roads should be quiet, which will definitely help us get there faster. I need to finish this and save my girl.

Grant's foot hits the gas, and the engine shoots to life. He pulls out of the parking lot, and we head out toward the highway, which will take us out of the city and into the quieter area just outside the main center of San Antonio. There's not much there from what I can tell on the mapping system.

Of course, he'd go to a place that's far from

civilization. My heart thuds when I think of Tia. What he's doing to her. *I'm coming, baby. Just hold on. I love you. I fucking love you. Don't you dare leave me.* My mind repeats the vow, the promise, the three words we'd both been too afraid to say, and I'm just praying it's not too late.

"We'll find her. She's going to be okay. Stop worrying so much." Grant's voice drags me from the concern that's taking over my mind.

"I know, man. It's just . . ." My words taper off, and I'm not sure what to say. How to say it. I've not confessed my love for her yet, but I know I can trust the man beside me.

"You love her, I know. We've had this conversation, Brax. You'll get to tell her. Mark my words," he says in a tone filled with conviction. If he's so sure, then so am I.

I'll find you, baby. I swear on my life, I'll find you.

the past

Tia

"There's my little girl." The familiar rumble of the man I ran from for so long wakes me from a dream of safety. Of Braxton. When my eyes crack, he's there. The Devil himself. Revulsion, fear, and anxiety hit me so hard my breathing stutters. I've been hanging from these ropes for so long, and my hands are numb, but all I want to do is wrap them around his neck.

My fingers tingle, and I swallow the bile that sits in my throat like a lump, threatening to choke me. Thankfully, Belle shoved some panties and a tank top on me before she left me here to die.

Pinning him with a glare, I don't respond, but fear slowly slithers like a serpent through me.

"Now, Belle has outdone herself. Finding

you and presenting you, so . . ." A thick finger trails its way up my bare hip, sending another wave of dread coursing through my veins. He snakes it around my head, and with a big, strong hand, he grips my hair roughly. "Beautifully."

A small squeak falls from my lips; it's all I can muster. My strength is depleted, and the pain from having my hair wrenched back has tears forming in my eyes, but I refuse to cry. I'll not give him the satisfaction of seeing my tears.

It's been years, and he still has the power over me to send me into panic. He's older but still evil. Dark eyes, almost black under thick dark brows, bore into me. The scar that runs from under his left eye down to his chin seems to glow in the dim light. That's the scar I gave him, and the memory has my body tingling to do it again. I'm only dressed in a skimpy top and a pair of panties, but the way he's looking at me, I might as well be naked. I feel bared to him, flayed open for his hungry gaze.

"Still such a feisty little thing, aren't you, Tia?" he hisses in my face, spittle flying from his mouth and landing on my cheek. It has more memories surfacing, choking me. My body quakes when he once again pulls me forward. My arms scream in agony from being tied up all this time. I don't know how long I've been here, but now, as the light turns a burnt orange, I would have to guess at least twelve hours. Unless . . . I've forgotten. I've gone *there*. "I'm going to make sure you pay for all the shit you caused with that little boyfriend of yours. Do you know he came into my club and tried to take me down?"

"No, I didn't." My thoughts falter when I think of Braxton.

I knew he was working for Retribution. They were the ones who saved me. Only Braxton doesn't know. I never told him my whole story. I never told him everything that made me who I am today.

I never told him if it wasn't for his boss, Corp, I wouldn't be alive. Corp and his team found me and told me where to find my father. Corp saved me from spending my whole life searching for a man who I knew would hide until the day he took his last breath.

"Of course you did, little Tia," he asserts with the confidence of the asshole he is. I didn't know about their plan to take my father down. If I did, it would have been easier for me to complete my plan and exact my revenge.

It's been years; too long has passed since I

vowed that I'd kill him. And now that I'm in the same room, I'm in no fucking condition to do it.

Break free.

I can't.

If you don't do it now, you'll never be able to.

How? Tell me how?

Get him to loosen your bindings.

He won't listen to me.

With the conversation playing in my mind, I watch him stalk around the room, pulling up a chair before me. The small silver tray he sets on the table beside me glints, stealing my attention from the war raging in my mind, and my gaze falls on the *tools* he's about to use on his youngest daughter.

You see, my father is a master of torture. Of hurting people. However, he's no longer the one they call when all else has failed. He's the one who now runs the show.

Master manipulator.

So are you.

She taunts me, telling me things I don't believe. *Can I really manipulate him into undoing my bindings? Into letting me go?* Perhaps. *But what then? I kill him and get put away for it?* I need to think. To figure out how this is going to play out.

"Tia, my baby girl." He commands my

attention, and when I meet those evil, dark eyes, I know there's no choice but to play along.

I need to give him something, play on his emotions. If there's one thing I know about him, it's that he's a man who's fueled by them. Growing up with him has given me an insight into the workings of his brain. "Father, can we talk? I have missed you. So, so much." My voice drops on the last few words as I pour sadness into it. My acting abilities must have worked, because he jolts in surprise.

"You missed me?" He laughs incredulously. "Do you miss the day you stood toe to toe with me and told me you were going to kill me?" His tone is filled with anger now. Good. Emotion. I need that to work with. If he's angry, it means I can weave my way into his head and make him release me.

"No." I drop my gaze again, hoping to hide my expression and not show fear. "I just . . . I was wrong when I said that. My fear overrode everything else, and I didn't realize what I was saying." The words I spew are bullshit, but I know I have him when his gaze softens.

If I convince him that I love him, he'll let me go, and I can finally get the revenge I need and want. He grips the smooth, steel blade from the tray. A scalpel that I know he can use to hurt me more than I'd like to admit. Or recall for that matter.

He shakes his head as he pushes up, rising to full height. Like that night when I broke, fear riddles my senses like a poison, slowly seeping into the cracks of who I am. Those shattered pieces that he created in me are now at his feet.

He holds all the cards. I'm fucked. "Look, you're here to hurt me," I level with him, my voice more confident and stronger than I expect, and from the look on his face, something he didn't expect either. "But, deep down, you know I'm the key to getting you out of whatever plan Brax and his team are working on." In the hopes that he listens and doesn't freak out, I watch as he contemplates my words.

My heart catapults into my throat, the beats hastening as his gaze darkens.

Thud. Thud. Thud.

Thud. Thud. Thud.

Shit.

You've fucked it up, Tia.

No. No. No.

Black swirls around me, threatening to engulf me, but I can't do this now. I can't lose sight of him in this moment. Please, please, don't. I beg and plead. And it seems to work momentarily. In seconds, my father, the Devil himself, is mere inches from me. "Do you think for one second I want *you* to help *me*?" He spits out the words like they're venomous.

"I just—"

"You just thought you could fuck over your old man. Why? Because you blame me for your fucked-up brain?" He laughs, the sound so dark and evil it's as if he drenched me in ice-cold water. My body shivers in the dim light, in the darkness of the room I've been hanging in. It's about the size of an office, with space I'd guess for a desk and chair, but it's only furnished with a sofa, which is situated opposite me. The same one where Ryker fucked my sister.

When I drag my blurry gaze back to him, I find my father's demented smirk pinned on me.

Black. Black. Black.

Kick him.

I can't.

Do something, Tia.

I can't.

You need to fight.

It's over. I don't have anything left in me. My body aches. He reaches out a hand, fisting my hair and tugging my head back. "My daughter, the two-faced little bitch. I gave you everything. I almost lost clients because of you and that stupid brain of yours." I wince in pain as his fingers grip my hair tighter, holding me in place so he can sneer into my face.

The strands in his grasp sting my scalp as the bite of pain shoots through me. "Please," I beg, one more try to make him see reason, but it's futile. When he's like this, there's nothing that can stop him. Nothing that can break down those black walls he has around him.

"Don't fucking speak." Then I feel it, the cold metal on my skin. He carves into me. The smooth flesh of my neck lacerated by the sharp blade. Slowly. Meticulously. Painfully. All the while I feel the blood trickle, drop by crimson drop, I go to my place.

That place. My haven.

Only this time, it's not *her* there. It's him. With piercing caramel eyes, he smiles.

Holding out a hand to me.

Braxton Carter.

The man my heart belongs to. The one person in this world I finally allowed myself to feel something for again. The only person I've loved since my mother.

Tears sting my eyes, threatening to spill. I

try to hold them back as the blade slices between my bared breasts. My chest heaves in agony, and I try to still my heart.

I want to leave this place. To wake up beside Brax, to feel his arms around me. Steadying me. Making me indestructible. Because as my own father etches the metal into my skin, marking me with this filth, it feels as if I'm breaking all over again.

All those fragments that Brax put together, all those tiny pieces he mended are coming undone, inch by bloodied inch, and I don't think I'll ever be whole again.

"Look how beautiful you are, Tia," Satan coos in my ear. Releasing his hold on my hair, he steps back and admires his handiwork. From my jaw all the way down to my belly button is a smarting sliver of red. I feel the lifeforce seeping from me. So slow it's almost unnoticeable. This is what he does. I've seen him do it too many times before.

You see, my father is an artist of sorts. He's got a steady hand. He moves swiftly. Making him an artist of torture, slicing open flesh, displaying his creations, using the bodies of his victims as canvases.

Now, he's made me a victim. I'm his

masterpiece. "Father." My voice is croaky. My eyes flutter closed as unconsciousness steals me, but I fight it. It's the only thing I can manage. All my strength bleeds from my wound along with the deep merlot-colored metallic fluid that now marks the floor below me. "Please . . . d-don't . . ." My mouth is dry as I beg for my life. The one slipping through my fingers. "D-do . . . t-this . . ."

He doesn't respond, only picks up another instrument from his torture tray and nears me. I can't see what it is. My vision blurs, and the tears I've kept at bay now fall. They tumble from my eyes and stream down my cheeks. The saltiness stings the wounds on my lips and face.

"You, my sweet little, Tia, are going to die. Do you know why? Because you're just like your mother. That's why I had to take care of her. You were too young for them to incarcerate, and your mental health wasn't one hundred percent, so you took the fall. And all these years you believed it. Didn't you?" he seethes in my ear.

My head is starting to spin. I have no more words. I slump forward, my head hanging like a limp rag doll. Pain sears me again and again, but somewhere in the darkness I find light.

I go to *him*.

Braxton.

I love you.

the past

braxton

The door flies open. It's dark inside, but I feel her. As if her magnetic force is pulling me closer. She's here. I can't just storm in, so when the two men in front lift their guns and head inside, I follow. My Glock is trained before me.

"Sir!" one of the men on my team bellows, and my heart bangs against my chest so hard I'm sure it's cracked a fucking rib. Entering the larger part of this house, I see him exiting through a doorway from what looks like a smaller room. When I reach it, I see her. *Tia.* I rush toward her and find her body hanging by a rope. There are small cuts and abrasions from her hips up her body to just under her breasts.

Blood has dried between her thighs and from the slashes on her smooth caramel skin, and everything in me fights to hold it together.

Her face is perfect besides the small cut on her cheek. Her lips are cracked, and all I want to do is kiss them until they're soft and pliable. I want to heal her. To fix her.

"Baby," I murmur, circling my arms around her waist as Grant cuts her down. As soon as she's loose, her arms fall to her sides, and she's now slumped in my arms. "Jesus, what have they done to you?" I murmur into her hair, inhaling her scent, mixed with the smell of blood. My rational thinking flies out the fucking window.

If that fucker was here now, I'd rip him apart. Limb by fucking limb.

Walking us backward, I slump on a worn sofa with her small body in my arms. It's then she mumbles in her semi-conscious state. "I love you, Brax." The words still my heart for a moment before catapulting it into my throat.

Men swarm around me, taking evidence and bagging it. Her breathing is ragged, and when the medics finally arrive, they scoop her up and place her on the gurney.

"Her heart rate is stable, but we'll need to get her back to HQ, Brax," one of the paramedics, I think his name is Lincoln, informs me.

"I'm riding along." I stalk out the door with them. But I feel a hand on my shoulder, stopping me. I turn to find Grant.

"She'll be okay. A strong woman doesn't go down easily." Nodding, I swallow the lump of emotion threatening to choke me and leave him with the rest of the team to collect all we need to put that fucker away.

My concern is for my girl. Her safety and well-being are now at the forefront of my mind, and until she's awake and telling us what happened, I will not be able to concentrate on anything. Fear for her life, and fear that I'll do something I might regret when I find that fucker burns through me.

Once I'm safely in the back of an unmarked vehicle, they take off toward our warehouse. To the safety that we're assured. I've made my choice. She's mine. And soon she'll know who I really am.

Not once over the almost twelve months I've known her have I been honest about what I do. I've deflected every time she's brought it up, but now the truth will come out.

Including hers. I need to know everything there is to know about the man she calls Dad. The one I'm going to put away for life. Fuck, who knows, perhaps I should put him down.

I watch them work on her wounds, cleaning

her cuts, but even with her skin bruised, sliced open, I see the girl I fell in love with. The woman I want in my life. Even though she's battered and contused, she's still beautiful. Perfect in every way.

The lacerations will leave scars, perhaps forever, and I know she'll remember this every time she looks in the mirror. I just hope the reminder will not hinder our journey together, and we'll be able to forge ahead, making sure our future is filled with happiness and not the sick memories of what happened to her.

Even those dark demons she hides in her mind.

The same ones she doesn't know I share.

It's been hours. My mind is racing with what they're doing. The doctor has been in there for too long. He's the best in the country, but deep in my gut, I'm filled with an emotion I've not let myself feel since I saw my parents lying in a pool of their blood.

Fear.

Anxiety fills me with dread. Frustration morphs into anger. The emotion that swirls inside me is like a hurricane storming a city, taking down everything in its path.

"Hey man?"

I turn to see my partner and friend stalking toward me. "Grant, how did it go? Any news?" Maybe he can take my mind off the shit running through it, the fear and worry.

"We found blood and semen samples in the room, which we tested." His words send ice racing through my veins. "The blood was Tia's. A lot of it. The other tests matched with Ryker's DNA. He's involved in this. The woman we saw him with was Tia's sister, Isabelle. We're not sure how or why she's involved, but I'm guessing it has to do with their childhood and her being sold into the sex trade. We've tracked down all the information. Corp wants to see you when you're done here," he informs me, speaking in a steady tone.

His words sink in, thick and slow, like molasses pulling me under. Ryker? Why is he doing this? My best friend. He was like a brother to me. And here he's on the wrong side, doing shit like this to a woman that I'm in love with.

My chest aches trying to make sense of everything. "So, Ryker's involved? What the fuck? He's on a downward spiral and decides to go fucking insane?" I bite out, and the man before me stills, watching me fall apart, but he doesn't touch me. Which is a good thing because I'd lose it. I'd fucking punch anything in my way right now. All I get is a nod. Swallowing the thick lump in my throat which threatens to suffocate me, I shake my head and ask, "What about Tia's sister?"

"There are reports that Miguel had auctioned his eldest daughter to his business associates. She was sixteen." The information has my stomach roiling in shock. What. The. Fuck? "Tia was never sold, however . . ." He stalls, and I want to grip him by the shoulders and shake the fucking information from him. "There are medical reports that were filed away, after her father paid for them to be. Tia suffered multiple injuries from the age of sixteen. It seems that this is when it started for both sisters. She's been seeing psychotherapists and psychologists since her twelfth birthday."

"But, I don't—"

"She believes she killed her mother. Only it wasn't her. She blacked out from the shock of seeing her mother murdered in cold blood. By her father. I have all the reports written up. The man who came forward with the information used to work for Miguel."

My mind is reeling, and nothing seems to make sense. At least to me.

"Why did he come forward now?"

"Miguel has his daughter. She's turning sixteen in four days' time," he offers, quieter this time.

Raking my hand through my hair, I inhale a deep breath, attempting to calm down, but it's futile because I'm livid. Anger slowly erupts from my core and travels its way through me as if I've been shot up with pure adrenaline.

"Jesus Christ, this man knows no bounds. No fucking limits," I growl out, rearing my fist, but before I can make contact with the wall, Grant's hand stops me. My anger is palpable, a living force swirling around me, ready to consume me like it's done so many times before.

Only this time, it's personal.

His gruff tone rumbles through the empty area where we're waiting. "You need to calm the fuck down, man. I know it's easier said than done, but you need to keep a level head here. This shit is going to eat you alive."

Concern is etched on his face, and the emotion swirling in his deep green eyes make them come alive as if a flame is dancing in them.

"She's in there because of that monster. His own daughter is fighting for her life because he's an animal. And you know what?" I turn to face him fully. "He should get slaughtered like the filth he is." With that, I stalk by the hulk of a man to grab my coffee from the table. Gulping the scorching drink, I savor the burn. It's the only thing that allows me to feel. I'm numb. Aching for her.

I've never been in love. Never wanted more than a one-night stand. I've never wanted to feel anything other than the agony of losing my parents, but somehow, when Tia walked, no, *stalked* into my life in those fuck off heels of hers, I was hooked. Like a junkie needing his next fix, I want her.

The satisfaction I got every time she pinned me with a furious stare, or curled her plump lips in frustration, or even when she finally submitted and allowed me to fuck her into oblivion, those were the times I was sated. Happy. And the blood that haunted my dreams and followed me seemed to ease, seemed to leave me, and I was finally in a place where I wanted more from life.

The chair screeches on the floor, and I turn to find my partner sitting back with his eyes shut tight. I take in the room and find the waiting area empty apart from Grant and me, and I'm thankful for that because I'm in no condition to have anyone else near me. The only thing I need right now is Tia.

To have her in my arms.

To see her glaring at me in frustration.

To see her come apart with my cock inside her.

To hear her whimper my name.

To mold my lips to hers.

To tell her I love her.

the present
Tia

"Do you remember the first time, Tia?"

Ignoring her question, I stare out the window. Does she really think something so horrid is easy to forget? She's silent, and I know she's waiting for me to tell her. To confide in her. But this, it's not something I can easily come out and confess. It's painful. It's horrific. It was the end of my innocence. It was the day my mind finally shattered. I'd always been broken, that much I knew. But it was this that finally broke the last shred of sanity I had.

And it was all my father's fault.

"Tia," she coos in a tone only a mother would use. It's melodic, calming, but it's not working on me. The darkness consumes me, and in my mind, I go back . . . back . . . back . . .

"It was so long ago. I remember Belle had

215

just gone, and I was left to fend for myself against him. There wasn't a day that passed by that he didn't hurt me. Both emotionally and physically."

"Did he ever . . .?" She tapers off, but I know what she wants. Shaking my head, I can't find the words, so it will have to do. "And do you know where your sister went?"

"Yes, I do now. Then, I didn't know. He told me she'd been sent away to a special school. I was only thirteen, so I didn't think anything of it." My focus is on the material of my jeans, the patterns and lines of the fabric is the only thing keeping me together. Focus. Calm. Breathe.

"And when did you realize it was a lie?" Good question. One I don't want to answer, but I know she'll prod and poke until I come clean. Until I tell her the ugly truth.

"It was the night she came back to me. When she returned as broken as I was. She was gone for so long I thought she had come to save me. But it was my father who broke us both."

I sit silently for a while, wondering what I can say to even get close to explaining what happened. But I can't. In the end, nobody will ever be able to comprehend the pain.

"I'd always known he did things that weren't

aboveboard, but it was one night that changed it all. It was really late, and I was woken up by a screech, so loud I'm sure the neighbors would have heard. I jolted upright, straining to hear where it was coming from, but then everything fell silent." My mind flits back to that night. I remember it like it was yesterday. As if no years have passed between me seeing what I did and experiencing the worst pain I've ever known.

"Tia?" she prompts.

"I pushed off the bed, padded to the hallway, slowly making my way to the basement. I knew my dad used to work down there, but he'd never allowed me in. The door was always locked, and I didn't dare go there because I was scared he'd catch me. As I neared the stairs, I heard sounds coming from behind the door."

I rise from the chair to turn toward the window. It's raining outside, and I savor the coolness of the glass, placing my hand on it.

"When I finally made my way down the staircase, I noticed the door was slightly ajar. The noises and voices were louder. But above all that, I heard crying, whimpering. Fear ricocheted through me as I felt my body tense. When I peeked around the door, that's when my world fell apart." Inhaling a deep breath, I shut my eyes so tight I see stars dancing behind them.

"And this was when you learned your father lied? Or . . .?"

Or . . .

"My father." A wry chuckle falls from my lips. "Yeah, Satan himself. The fucking Devil," I confess. Pain, so fucking acute, hits me in the chest. "I couldn't save her." More truths stumble from me like a dam bursting when I turn to face the woman who's been there all this time. Through everything, she's the only one who understands.

"Tell me, Tia." Once again, she pushes. Coaxing me to tell her the ugliness I witnessed. To let the truth out. To admit what broke me in the first place. I've never once admitted it. Never voiced it out loud.

"My father, along with three of his henchmen . . ." I can't look at her when I tell her, so I turn toward the dreary sky. "He was whipping a girl. She must have been sixteen. His friends had her hands on their cocks. Fisting hard as steel while they watched with demonic eyes as my father hurt her." It's only when I reach up to my face that I realize I'm crying. "I watched them mutilate her. I watched. I didn't do a fucking thing because I was too fucking scared." I hiss out the words. Anger. Guilt. Shame. All those emotions barrel through me, and I fall to my knees. "They killed her, and I didn't do a fucking thing." The words are muffled because I can't form them anymore.

"Tia." Her voice is close, right at my ear. Her arms encircle me, holding me against her chest. Warmth seeps through me, but I'm left cold and stranded in my mind. "You were a little girl," she once again murmurs softly. She's trying to make me feel better, but it's not going to work.

I am responsible.

I should have stopped them.

I could have screamed.

Called the police.

But I stood in shock. My legs didn't want to carry me away.

Blood.

There's always blood.

"Please, help me," I beg, plead, lifting my face to meet her eyes. Those sweet, caring eyes that have guided me my whole life.

"I'll always be here for you, Tia," she promises, but I know she's lying. She can never be here for me again.

"I love you, Mom."

the past
Tia

Everything hurts.
Open your eyes.
I can't.
You can. You're safe.
No. No. He's here.
Open your eyes.
Stop. Just stop.
Do you feel it? Feel him?

The question stills our conversation, and I try to concentrate. Feel him? What does she mean? Calming my mind, I inhale deeply. I shiver; I'm cold. My body aches; my bones feel as if they've been frozen, as if I've been sitting in a refrigerator. A consistent beep comes from my right, and silence sits on my left. It's bright. Even though my eyes are closed, I can see a white light.

Beep. Beep. Beep.

Another sound catches my attention. Hissing, whooshing, something . . .

Open your eyes, Tia.

She coaxes again.

Beep. Beep. Beep.

Come on, baby girl. You've spent too long in the dark.

Find your light.

Find him.

He's waiting . . .

Her voice fades, and my eyes finally crack open. It's too bright, and I wince in pain. A groan, low and gravelly, rumbles in my throat. I try to swallow it down.

"Tia," a concerned, yet familiar voice, calls to me. "Baby, please open your eyes. I'm here."

His murmur is filled with love. *Love*? Shit.

"Where . . .?" The word scrapes against my throat, which has my eyes pricking with tears. *How am I in so much pain? What happened?*

"Tia, I'm here. It's Brax," he whispers over my cracked, dry lips. I must look like shit. "Can you hear me, Vixen?" This time, his mouth is near my ear, which sends goosebumps skittering across my skin. Opening my eyes, I glance around the stark room. When my gaze meets his concerned one, I find emotion that sends me into turmoil.

It's right there, leaving me breathless.

Love.

"Brax?" My voice is raspy, and my throat burns when I attempt to talk. Everything aches. The only thing I feel is pain, everywhere. "What . . . Where am I?"

"You're safe now. We found you in a warehouse. You were unconscious," he murmurs so quietly I can barely hear him. As if he's down a tunnel, and I'm on the other end. "Tia." My name on his lips is filled with need. Concern is etched on his handsome face, furrowing his brows and darkening his gaze. He reaches for my face, stroking it tenderly as if I'm made of glass. "We ran tests. You're going to be okay."

I release a breath I didn't know I was holding. The pain that is present over my body is mind-numbing. "Brax." My voice is unrecognizable. "It's R-Ryker . . ." He nods. Of course they've figured it out already.

"We've found out a lot more than we bargained for, but what's important right now, Tia . . . you need to tell me about your father." I knew this would be something he'd need to know.

I ignore his question, countering with one of my own. "How long have I been in here?" For a long moment, he stares at me, and then he drops his gaze to my hands where the tubes are attached to needles. I can practically see the wheels in his head turning. The only thing I want to do is feel his warmth, to be cocooned in his arms.

"Three days." Dragging those caramel orbs back to my blue ones, he watches my reaction as if I'm the most interesting thing in the room.

"You knew he was my father?" I murmur, gesturing with my hand to my chest. The needle in my arm pinches, and I can't help wincing. I've been through far worse. I don't know why this is getting to me. But after what he did to me in that warehouse while I was chained, I'm surprised I'm alive.

A shudder wracks through me involuntarily, and I meet his concerned eyes. "Yes, the night you found me in your living room, I knew." I stare at him for such a long time. The heaviness in the room is stifling. He knew who I was, and he still wanted me? I don't understand.

"Why did you stay?" I ask.

His gaze meets mine and heats me in the coolness of the room. "You know why, Tia. Or did you want me to tell you word for word?"

Do I? Would it heal my mind if someone said it? Those three words. Shrugging, I lean back and watch him. His hair is mussed, as if he'd just woken up. There are also dark circles under his eyes, and his clothes are crumpled.

"Did you sleep here?" I question, needing to fill the silence, but not wanting to tell him I so desperately need to hear the words.

He nods. Nearing the bed, he leans in and reaches for my hand. His eyes pierce my soul.

"Tia, I'm in love with you." Six words that steal my breath. Gold eyes glisten with unshed tears, the sincerity in them shining through as if I'm looking through a window. His soul is there, calling to mine. We need each other to survive. It's clear now. I'll never be without him. For some reason, he loves me, wants me. And as much as I'd like to push him away and save him from me, my mind, and everything else, I'm going to be selfish. I'm going to walk with him into the dark. I just hope he's strong enough to pull me out.

"I'm in love with you too, Brax." My confession has my heart leaping into my throat and my stomach fluttering with anxiety. I've never loved anyone before.

"I know, you told me before." One side of

his mouth lifts infinitesimally, it's the smallest smirk, but on him it lights up his whole face.

"What?" I squeak.

He nods slowly, chuckling at the memory that I don't have. "When I carried you from the warehouse, you murmured it while you were in my arms."

"Oh, God," I groan in embarrassment. I was so drugged; I didn't know what was happening or where I was. I must have been dreaming.

"Look, we'll talk about that soon, but what's more important is what your father wanted from you and what your sister has to do with all this?"

Questions.

Questions.

Tell him, Tia.

No. I can't.

You can't hide forever. He'll find out. One way or another.

"My sister hates me. She believes it's my fault she was sold and taken away. My father told her I chose for her to go instead of me. She thinks I killed our mother, but to be honest, I don't know if I did or didn't. It's all a memory that's locked so deep in my subconscious that I've never been able to recall it. I came to San Antonio to find him. Innuendo was registered in his name, and it was my only link to finding him and making him pay for what he did. All the secrets are unravelling before me, and I don't know what to do, Brax." I sneak a glance at him, hoping he doesn't run the other way, but he shocks me by nodding.

"Your mental condition is what's shielding you from it. You need to let go of the place you run to in your mind, and you'll be able to focus on the real memories."

The serious tone of his voice stills me for a moment. "What? How do you—?"

"I went through the same thing you did, Tia." His gaze bears down on mine, watching for something. Recognition. He's like me. Broken.

"But—"

"I saw your medical files, Vixen. I know about you, your mind. It's going to be okay. This will all be over soon, and we'll go away. Okay?" Confidence in his words, surety in his eyes, love in his smile, it all slams into me, leaving me breathless. Nodding, I turn away, but his fingers reach for my chin, making me look at him again.

"Don't run from me. I'm not leaving, and I don't want you going anywhere. We're in this together. Tia, since the first day I saw you, I felt you" — he places my hand on his chest — "in here." My vision blurs, and when I blink, all the emotion from the past hits me as if a dam has burst, and I can't hold back anymore.

Somehow, he manages to shift his way onto the hospital bed beside me, and he cradles me. My body wracks with shivers and sobs. He doesn't tell me it's going to be okay. All he does is hold me and allow me to purge all the pain and anger.

I don't know how long we sit there, but when the tears finally stop, Braxton moves and regards me. "We're going to get revenge, Vixen. I'll make sure of it," he promises. His vow grips my heart and tears spring to my eyes.

"Thank you, Brax. I'm ready to kill him. The time has come to end this." My own pledge is enough for him, and I get that smile. The one he always gives me. The one that makes my heart fill with want, need, and love.

"Then that's what we'll do."

the past

We're outside the warehouse where Miguel is meant to be holed up. I've got a team behind me, Tia and Grant on either side flanking me. We've taken four days to plan this, but I know for a fact that Miguel Alvarez is not stupid. He's not someone who's going to sit back and wait for us to come at him.

"Are you sure you're ready?" I ask Tia.

She nods. Her body has healed quickly, but her mind is still broken. I see her thoughts drift, and when they do, I'm here to bring her back. I'm her anchor as much as she is mine. I don't know if this is going to help her or not, but revenge is something we both need.

Slowly, we make our way through the dark building. My heart thuds, echoing in my ears. I wonder if anyone else can hear it. Can she? Does she know how much I want this to be over so I can finally be with her?

"Brax?" she whispers quietly, and I turn to her. "Thank you for doing this. I . . ." Her words taper off, and those ice-blue eyes lower to the gravel below our black combat boots. Whenever she turns away from me, it feels as if my world tips off its axis. As if she's my moon, and I'm her tide.

The Retribution team behind us is armed and ready for any shit that arises. I've told them she comes first. I don't want anything happening to her. Not again.

"I would do anything for you. That's how this works, Tia." The honesty in my tone is clear. This is what I want. She is who I want. The decision was easy. When I told Corp I was ready to move on, he was supportive and gave me everything we needed to take Tia's father down once and for all.

As we enter the main area of the vast metal warehouse, the lights flicker on, and we're surrounded by men with guns. They're trained on us, and fear grips me. My chest is tight, and my heart is about to break its way through my fucking chest.

"Ah! My daughter and her boyfriend.

Welcome." Miguel Alvarez steps forward, his filthy, leering gaze on Tia. I want to rip his eyes out. I know what he did to her when she was bound and helpless. She'll forever have the scars to remind her. Not that she was taken and hurt, but that she was strong and survived. That's what I remind her every day. I don't want to think about what he did when she was a child.

Bile rises in my throat, burning with need to spew on this monster.

"I told you I'd kill you one day. Today is that day, Father." My girl's stare is venomous, her words laced with hatred, and I don't blame her.

A loud guffaw falls from his lips as he regards her.

"Don't be silly, child. You were always one for theatrics. I suggest you all drop your weapons. My men will be storing them away safely." He turns to walk farther into the bowels of hell, and we follow.

But before I can take a step forward, I'm ripped back by the collar of my shirt. "Gun!" A grunt from behind me has anger threatening to take hold. Spinning on my heel, I strike the fucker behind me. Two others step forward, grabbing my arms, and I'm met with Ryker's dark glare. "Hitting your best friend? That's no way to greet me, Brax." He chuckles, bringing his gun up and hitting me across the face with it.

Tia's scream echoes around me, and then I hear her father again. "Bring my daughter." And with that, I'm dragged, along with Tia, leaving my men behind with guns trained on them.

We're taken into a room lit only by a single bulb hanging from the ceiling. "Sister."

I turn to find an older version of Tia staring at us. Her hair is long and wavy with golden highlights. Everything about her physical appearance is like my girl except her eyes—her hair, her face, even her skin tone could be Tia. They could be twins, but I can tell the difference. What separates Tia from her sister is the strength and fight in her heart.

"This is a good-looking man you've got yourself, little sister. Does he know what a whore you are?" She cackles evilly, stalking toward me. Dressed in a tiny leather skirt and a black tank top that pushes her tits up, she nears me. Leaning in, she grips my chin, and tilts my head to the side with the strength of a man. She runs the tip of her nose up my neck, inhaling me. "Mmm, so delicious. I think I may have to figure out why my sister is so infatuated with you." Her lips brush against mine, and I shudder in revulsion.

"Get the fuck away from me," I growl.

"Oh now, don't be so picky. Just ask Ryker. I'm a good fuck. Maybe you and Ryk can take me at the same time." Her deep laugh surrounds me. I have to bite back my anger.

"Just let us go. We're—"

"Enough!" Miguel bellows, dragging our attention away from his eldest daughter. "It's time for Braxton and me to get acquainted. Since my little girl wants to be with him, I need to make sure he's worthy of her. Bring him into the office," he orders the two men. They obey, dragging me toward a small, dark, dank-smelling room. Shoving me into a chair, they bind my arms and legs, and then leave the room. "So, Braxton Carter, the man who thought he could fuck with my business. Do you know why I've been doing this for so long?" He leans in, his face inches from mine.

"Because you're a fucking asshole who's been lucky," I taunt, met with a dark chuckle from the man before me.

"Lucky? I am a legend!" Gripping my neck, he tugs me closer, ensuring the restraints burn into my wrists. "You see, Braxton," he spits my name, "I'm going to kill you. Slice you from ear to ear. And you know what the best part will be? My fucking whore of a daughter watching her boyfriend bleed to death."

"You can kill me, you can do anything you'd like to do, but let me tell you one thing. Tia is stronger than you think. She will kill you." His guffaw booms through us, but I continue. "She's no whore. She's a woman."

His fist answers for him, smashing painfully into my face. My eyes lose focus, and I see black

. . .

"Braxton, wake the fuck up!" Grant's deep voice drags me from the dark. I crack my eyes. "Man, you better look at me." His warning has me rousing. When I meet his gaze, my heart leaps into my throat.

"What? Where is she?" He's tugging at my wrists, and my arms fall to my sides. The blood rushes through my veins, and the tingling sensation wakes my limbs from their slumber. "What happened?"

"He knocked us both out. They've got Tia. We need to get in there," he whispers carefully, his eyes darting to the door. Mine follow. It's flimsy. The lock doesn't look like it can withstand much.

"Do you think Corp has a second team on

the way?" I ask. Grant nods. I know my boss, and he's always got a backup. A light shining through the small window close to the ceiling catches my attention. Then I hear it. Gunshots.

"Corp brought Team Two in, we—" My partner's words fall away when I push to my feet and storm the door. With my adrenaline pumping wildly through my veins, I shoulder it open and find Miguel holding Tia with a knife at her throat.

"Get down!" he orders, but the chaos in the warehouse takes hold, and the noise is bearing down on me. My girl's gaze flits around, taking in the commotion. I'm about to rush them when I hear one resounding shot, and I see them both collapse. Everything plays out in slow motion. The large metal gate is bashed in, and more of the men I trained with swarm the area, taking out Miguel's brutes. I race to Tia's side.

"Baby?" When she glances up at me, there's only one emotion in her eyes. Revenge. We both dart for Miguel who's limping away, but he's wounded and doesn't get far. Gripping his neck, I tug him back, and he stumbles. "Time for some revenge, don't you think, Tia?" I ask, and she smiles. It's not her sweet, innocent smile she always gifts me, but one filled with the desire to kill. Hunger to annihilate the man I'm dragging toward the rope hanging from the ceiling.

My woman stalks up to me with unfathomable strength. We work knots around Miguel's wrists, and with the help of Grant, we heave him up and latch the rope to a hook in the ceiling. The energy in the room is electric. We've got the asshole, and he's not getting away again. No more women will be hurt. No child will ever be maimed by this piece of trash.

Moments later, with the help of some of the men, I look toward her, and I see it.

I'd call it a vision.

A dream come true.

Revenge in its best form.

Miguel is bound, bleeding, hanging from the high ceiling by the metal chains I asked them to bind him with. Tia kneels, gripping the handle of a long, sleek blade—the same one he used on her. She wields it back and forth, and the glint shimmers in the low light from the bulb. "Baby?" I call to her, but she doesn't hear me. It's as if she's in another world. Her world. The place where she's safe from him and the evils that have haunted her for so long.

As much as I'd like my own revenge, this is more than I could have ever asked for. My woman is about to exact her revenge, and I want a fucking front-row seat.

Her hand reaches up, and the silver glints in the low light. I watch it as she slices from his ear to his neck. Blood trickles and dots his dark skin, and I watch it drip, slow and steady. His loud chuckles vibrate through every inch of the space. Dark and evil.

"Father, it's been a long time coming, but today, you'll pay." Her voice is dark and sinister, and when I reach her, she drives the knife into his thigh. She twists it so slowly I feel the twinge in my leg. "You feel that, Daddy?" she bites out in anger. I don't notice it until I see her other hand move. Another sharp blade slices at his shirt, and it falls away.

"You can't kill me, little Tia, you love me," he growls with poison dripping from his tone.

"Love? Love!" Her voice is shrill, and when I place a hand on her shoulder, her head twists toward me, and her eyes meet mine. With a dark smirk, she hands me the knife and steps back. "He killed your parents," she informs me with confidence. I turn my cold, hate-filled gaze on the man in question.

"Of course I did. That fucker didn't help me when I needed it most. A lawyer? He was a fucking nobody," the evil piece of shit shouts, and my blood boils.

"Fuck you!" I growl and sink the knife that was handed to me into his stomach. A gurgle falls from his mouth, but even then, a sinister smirk is present on his face. When I finally step back, I watch my girl take the lead. She carves into the skin of the man she calls father.

"Do you remember, Daddy?" she spits his name. "When you forced your fist into my body, when I cried and screamed?" With every word, she slices into his skin. The merlot color drips from the wounds on his torso and pools on the floor below him, creating a thick, almost black puddle; his eyes flutter closed.

She recalls scenes from her childhood. She recollects the moments her innocence was stolen. She tells him about the day her body bled for days. With each story, my blood boils, and it heightens to the point of pain.

"You loved me," he argues, and suddenly, she rears her fist back, and it slams into his jaw.

A loud crack resounds from his face, and blood oozes from his nose. "I fucking hated you, every moment of my life." With that, she glances at one of the men on my team and points to the canister of gas he's carrying. I know we'd planned on burning this place down, but what she does next leaves me speechless. Gripping the handle, she douses him in the strong-smelling liquid. "Now, you'll burn in hell for what you did. For raping me, selling me, for making me a whore." Before anyone can get near her, she lights the match, and the man she calls father lights up in flames.

"Tia." My voice is thick with emotion. Shock.

"It's over now." She turns to me and meets my eyes with a sadistic smile. "Take me home."

And I do.

the present

Tia

The room is exactly the same as it always is. Light streams through the blinds, warming me in the chair opposite her. She's smiling. It's a smile I've seen since I was young. I remember it so clearly, as if all this is real. "Tia, it's time for you to leave. Are you happy to be walking away from this place now?" she asks.

Glancing around, I take in the paintings, the dark wood desk, even the fish tank that sits against the wall beside the bookshelves.

"I'll miss you," I tell her honestly, because I will. My whole life I've been alone. I've been hidden in a world by myself. My mind had been split in two. I suffered from Bicameralism, where one part of my brain "spoke" to the other, and the second part would listen and obey.

When I killed my father, I broke, shattered

even. I was no longer just crazy; I was completely locked away in the world I'd made up. I've spent a year talking, telling my story. Brax and I healed each other, but he is my anchor to this world. He's the one that keeps me in this reality.

That's why when he told me he wanted to take me home, I agreed. There was nothing more that I could want than to be his wife one day. To have his children. They tested me when I was brought in, and my body had healed in a way that would allow me to carry a baby. When I was younger, my father's doctors told me I'd never be able to have children. They told me I was broken.

"And you've told him everything?" She grins with pride on her beautiful face, and I nod. He knows everything. He knows about how I attacked the barmaid in the club when I found Ryker fucking her. He watched me, saved me from doing something stupid. Braxton had to rip me off her, but not before I got my claws into her pale flesh. "What about Laney?" My best friend, or only friend, who had turned out to be a spy for my father.

"Braxton did a background check when I went missing. He remembered her from the nightclub and found out she was put in place by Miguel and Isabelle to keep an eye on me." My heart hurt so much at that. Apparently, her boyfriend was one of my father's men. I recall his nickname for me now and why I hated it so much. His father used to call me that when he . . . when he was at our house, raping me. He hurt me more than I had ever imagined. The first man to make me bleed besides my father, of course. My subconscious obviously remembered the word, Pussycat, but not the reason why I hated it so much.

"That was the last time I saw her, at the nightclub," I confess. "Braxton has been searching for her, but I have a feeling my father may have gotten to her."

She nods again. Pushing off the chair, she walks over to the cabinet and opens it. Lifting something, she turns and holds it out to me. It's a photo. Her, Belle, and me. I remember when it was taken. Just before she was brutally murdered by my father.

"I love you, Tia, but it's time for you to go now. Live your life. You don't need me anymore." Her voice is sad, filling my heart with a similar emotion. I want to mourn her. To cry and wail. To drop to my knees and beg her to stay. But I know I can't. It is time for me to go.

"I love you too, Mom. I'll always remember you," I promise, and she nods.

"I'll always be here . . ." She presses her fingers to my chest where my heart is, and I blink, allowing the tears to fall. "Goodbye, my Tia."

the present

"Are you sure she's ready? She's not going to lose it?" I ask the doctor.

He nods. "She'll have moments of confusion, but you're there. You're her grounding anchor."

Shaking my head, I recall how my girl's eyes lit up when I told her we were going home. The day I walk out of here with her has finally come, and it's the happiest fucking day of my life.

When she finally killed her father, her mind snapped. It was as if a cord had been cut, and we had to bring her in. Every day, I've been in this hospital, in this ward where they keep other mental patients, because of her, because of us. Retelling her everything about us and what happened, I waited with bated breath until she'd finally looked at me the way she did before her mind retreated into a world she'd created to escape. She doesn't know or remember when we first met as clearly as she once did. If I were her, I would block it out as well. But all those times I sat in the stark room telling her our story, she let the words permeate her mind.

Now that her father is dead, we've managed to bring down his organization. Hundreds of workers, men that had helped him sell girls, drugs, and weapons were either killed when they attempted to flee, or they're sitting in a maximum-security prison. We freed many girls. Corp had them housed in an old school where they're learning to read, write, and work. Learning life skills that they'd never been taught.

Isabelle was locked up along with Ryker for kidnapping my girl, among other charges that have put them away for life. The crimes that they've both had filed against them are horrific. It's sad to see Tia's sister spiral that far down and hit rock bottom. Her father's influence took over, and he created a monster by using his oldest daughter as a bargaining chip.

When Team One took the warehouse where Miguel was being held, Corp had a backup, which I didn't know about. If it weren't for him, both Tia and I would be dead. Now that we're free of the evil of her family, and this place that's kept her in something resembling a goddamned padded cell, I'm going to make sure her life is as normal as it can be.

I want the white picket fence and the children; I even want a damn dog.

It's been a long year for her, the therapy sessions, the medication, and I even ended up doing time with the psychologist to understand her mental health as well as mine. Yes, Tia will need constant care, but I'll be there for her. No matter what.

Now that my girl is ready to walk out of here with her mind intact, I'm ready to take her and make her mine. Marry her.

When they told me it was time to leave, that she was ready to be released, I knew what I had to do. I planned and made sure that we had a place to go. Somewhere we can call home. Her body is so fragile, almost as delicate as her mind after everything we've been through, *she's* been through, but she needs to live her life now.

I step into her room and find her standing at the suitcase I brought this morning. "It's time for us to go home, Tia." She nods with a smile. I've waited for this day for twelve long months.

Every day, I spent by her side.

Waiting. Watching. Needing.

We've been through our story.

She's been through therapy.

We've both learned to be around each other, with each other, and she's finally able to stop hiding from me. Her mind has stopped running, disappearing into that fucking fake world.

She's here with me now, and I'm not letting her go anywhere near that darkness. There was nothing I could do before but be by her side and pray to all the Gods there are that she holds onto me, rather than whatever she had within her.

As I recollected our story, I watched her come alive. Those beautiful eyes regarded me with more than affection; they looked at me with love. I told her everything that happened, the bad and the good. I told her how her smile would shine through my dark fucking thoughts. I spilled my heart to bring her back to me.

Honesty was best with her. I even told her about the time I woke up to find her screaming and thrashing in bed. I managed to roll her over and pin her down. She had a nightmare and freaked out. I learned all her secrets. I found out that her father had led both girls to believe they killed their mother.

The stories I heard about when she was a child and what he did to her made me want to dig up his burnt corpse and kill him over and over again.

She pads over to me wearing white ballet flats, which makes her shorter than me. She fits into my body perfectly. In sync, like we've been made, built to fit together.

"Brax, I'm ready," she breathes against my lips as she reaches up to kiss me. The sweet scent of her breath fans over my face, and my mouth waters to taste her. To devour her. She's no longer broken, no longer fragmented. She'll be mine forever.

"I know you are, baby, and I've never been happier."

She walks us backward toward the small desk in the room. "Sit, I'm going to pack." She smiles, a glimmer of happiness flickering in her gaze like a flame. Sitting back, I cross my arms in front of my chest and regard her with a smirk. She flies around the room, gliding from the closet to her bed, from her bed to the bathroom, and back again. Since there's not much to pack, she's done in twenty minutes. "That's it," she announces happily.

Her body has healed quickly, but I wonder briefly if her mind will remain fixed. I see her thoughts drift, and when they do, I'm here to bring her back. I'm her anchor as much as she is mine.

"Thank you, Brax," she murmurs as she drops her clothes into a suitcase bound for heaven. Where we can finally be together.

"I want to take you away, Vixen," I murmur quietly. My heart aches to see her like this. The medication I have to give her will ensure she can live a half normal life. And that's what I want. Being in this place for so long wasn't helping her, and I realized I couldn't do this anymore, so I told them I'd like to take her away. To take her home.

I love her. I've always loved her. She's been mine since the first day I saw her, and there's nothing that's going to keep us apart again.

"B-but . . . I-I . . .," she mumbles, shaking her head and gripping the material of her dressing gown until her knuckles are white. *Fuck.*

"Vixen?" At her nickname, her eyes dart to mine. With all the sessions we've spent together and with the story I told her about us, I want her happily ever after to come true. I wish with all I am that I could make her dream a reality. She believes I'm a gifted storyteller.

After witnessing her mother's brutal murder, her mind couldn't take it. Then, when her father and his filthy friends started abusing her, there was no telling the further damage that did to her psyche.

"Braxton?" I nod, and she smiles. The one thing I've been waiting for since I walked into this hospital today. "Take me home," she begs. Her soft pleas are enough to settle my resolve, and I open my arms. She rushes toward me, wrapping her arms around me and holding on as if I'm her lifeline. And I am.

"We're going home, baby," I whisper into her hair. The long, dark locks are curled today, and they smell of her sweet shampoo. I love how she feels in my arms, and I never want to have her stray from them.

It's been more than two years since I first laid eyes on her, and my need for this woman hasn't changed. It's only gotten stronger.

My heart is hers.

My soul is hers.

As hers are mine.

We belong together. I've never been surer of anything in my whole life.

Lifting her, I carry her through the doorway and down the corridor.

The new medication the doctor gave me in case I need it is meant to calm her episodes. Her mind is still lost in that place at times, with those memories, but with time, each pill she takes will wean her from the paracosm she's created.

I can only hope as we walk into our new life together, she'll finally walk away from it and be with me. When we reach the car, I settle her in the passenger seat and make sure the bags are in the trunk.

Sliding into the driver's seat, I rest my hand on her thigh before starting the car. I'm finally taking her to the home I purchased two months ago. With the guys helping me move in, I'm excited for her to see it.

She's silent as I weave the car through the grounds and out onto the road. It's not easy for her to be out of this place. The fear of something happening that could jar her mind is something we need to be careful of. It's not going to be easy, but I'll be by her side no matter what.

"The sun is so bright today," Tia says as she smiles.

She's right; there aren't any clouds in the sky. A perfect day. The closer we get to the suburbs, the more serene it becomes. Leaving behind the sterile hospital is like walking away from the past.

"It's your day," I tell her. "We'll have a picnic

in the garden. I can't wait for you to see the house." I haven't showed her photos. I wanted her first glance at our new home to be as exciting as if it were Christmas morning.

"I don't know what I would've done if I hadn't met you," Tia tells me. Her voice lowering, and I can hear the catch in her breath when she speaks. I've learned all her tells.

"You would've been strong on your own," I respond. "But I would've still found you. One way or another."

"Why?"

"Because you were made for me. I was always going to stumble across your path, and when I did, I would've stolen you for my own." I cast a quick glance her way and find her grinning at me.

"Oh really? You would've stolen me?"

"Yeah." I nod. "You know that you can never get away from me now. You're bound to me in more ways than one."

She responds with a smile and a blush. Her cheeks have a soft, rosy hue that makes every inch of my body stand to attention. I focus back on the road. I wanted to stop near the water, overlooking the ocean before I asked her the one question that's been on the tip of my tongue for a year now.

I wanted to wait until she was ready. We ride in comfortable silence until Tia flicks the radio, and we're serenaded by some pop song I don't really recognize. As the road leads closer to our destination, Tia sings along, taking in the scenery as I drive.

Her voice is melodic, in tune with whoever the artist is. I'm not sure how she even knows the lyrics, but she does.

We've been driving for almost two hours when we finally get glimpses of the ocean ahead. Tia's excitement is bubbling through her as she bounces on the seat when I finally pull up to the waterfront.

Corpus Christi.

I pull into a parking garage and kill the engine.

"This is where we're staying?" she questions in confusion, but I shake my head.

"No, come." I exit the vehicle and make my way around to the passenger side. Helping Tia from the car, I lead her to the pathway that snakes around the edge of the water.

In the slowly darkening sky, I notice how the city lights are flickering on. And that's when I drop down to one knee and pull out the small, black velvet box I've been holding onto for far too long.

"Tia, you came into my life and broke down every wall I built up. You keep telling me you're broken, but if you are, then so am I. And that's why I want to ask you to spend the rest of your life with me, so we can be two imperfectly broken pieces creating a new perfectly whole life together."

The tears that brim in her eyes melt my heart. I'm not a man who enjoys, or even attempts, romance. I'm a trained killer. But when I see my beautiful Vixen's tears, I can't help but want to chase them away.

"I-I never expected to ever feel happiness," Tia tells me earnestly. "But you've brought me back from the darkness that held me hostage for so long. You scared me when we first met." A small giggle falls from her lips before she continues, "I realized that you were someone who could possibly see through my cracked façade and love me anyway."

"I do. I love you so much, Vixen."

Another smile, this time bigger, brighter, and she nods before she finally answers, "Of course, I'll marry you."

"Then it's settled," I tell her as I slip on the

white gold, diamond ring I bought. "You'll be mine, forever, Mrs. Carter."

epilogue
Tia

One year later

The room is darker than the one at the hospital. Each movement flickers in my peripheral as if I'm not alone. "Tia." Jolting at the sound, I turn to find him. Smiling, I lift my hand and reach for him. He's carrying my tray of medication and a glass. Each day I take these, and with every pill, my mind doesn't wander. It doesn't go *there*.

"Brax," I quip playfully, which earns me a smile unlike any other. He's handsome. So devastatingly beautiful that sometimes it hurts to look at him.

He hands me the pill and water, which I take graciously, swallowing it down. I place the glass beside me and regard him again.

"How are you feeling?" he asks in a gentle tone filled with emotion.

"Tired." I lean back against the soft pillows and watch as he settles on the bed beside me. "Do you think we'll ever be normal?" The question comes out of nowhere, and I expect him to tell me no, that I'll never be able to have a normal life. I'm twenty-nine, and I've never been on a real date. I've known Braxton a long while now, and in that time, he's taken me on *dates*, but they weren't real. We spent our year in a hospital where I had to be for treatment. So I could heal and come back to him after the horrors I faced.

My mind is a tricky place.

The reality I made up while I was locked inside has given him an insight into the workings of my brain. In the time he spent with me in the hospital, he would visit me, talk to me, tell me the story I had shoved into the recesses of my mind. And as he did this for me, we found something real. We both fell more in love than I ever thought possible.

He's become my other half. He fills the broken parts of me and makes me feel whole again. And dare I say it—*normal*. It's something I never expected.

At first, falling in love with him felt as if I

was caught in the eye of a storm, or a tornado, just spinning without a safety net. It scared me. I was petrified at how he made me feel. But over time, I realized that if I just let him hold onto me, I would be grounded. And that's where I am right now.

For a whole year, twelve fucking months, while I sat in a hospital gown in a white room, Braxton sat beside me and told me a story. Our story. He recalled every moment. Our fairytale may have been unconventional, but I know that I'd never trade it for anything else. It's perfect as it is.

This is our story.

"Baby, listen to me." He cups my face in his hands and smiles. "We are perfect. You and me. We're incredible together. We're indestructible. Nothing will ever get in the way of our love, our lives. You are mine, Vixen," he vows, and my heart thuds. Excitement skitters, and my body responds. Needy and achy for my fiancé.

"I love you, Brax. I've been through the darkness of my past every day with my doctor. He's given me ways of working through it, but what's made me better was you. Us. With you telling me how we got here. That's what matters. I've been outside my mind, and inside, and nothing could ever have prepared me for the happiness you've brought to my life. But—"

My words are interrupted when his thumb traces my lower lip. It's a slow movement that heats my body. I'm always turned on and ready for him. I want him. I need him. And after what I have to tell him, I think he'll feel the same.

"Braxton, you're going to be a father," I whisper the words against his thumb, and our gazes meet. I found out not long ago that I'm pregnant. Because of my medication, I had to have regular tests. When I walked into the doctor's office two days ago, I didn't realize my life was about to change. He called me with the results and told me I should come in immediately. I arrived flustered and stressed, only for him to tell me I was going to have a baby. All those months in the hospital, and only when I was released did a miracle happen. Even though it wasn't planned, the smile that meets my worried stare is answer enough.

"I fucking love you," he hisses with hunger as his mouth devours mine.

forbidden series
other reads

Do you like it dark and emotional?

The Forbidden Series will take you on a journey as we meet the first two couples in this series. Kael and his Phoenix, as well as Samael and his Angel tread murky waters to find love, but in the darkness that surrounds them, there is always light.

From the Ashes (Book 0.5)

US: http://amzn.to/2izNLf6
UK: http://amzn.to/2iuqHf7
AU: http://amzn.to/2iGxrGz
CA: http://amzn.to/2iuiWps
iTunes: http://apple.co/2uLpzNG
Kobo: http://bit.ly/2ix4eBl
B&N: http://bit.ly/2h8cPut

Crave (Book 1)

US: http://amzn.to/2lnqO0C
CA: http://amzn.to/2mBB4Te
AU: http://amzn.to/2lnk9U9
UK: http://amzn.to/2lIg1dJ
Kobo: http://bit.ly/2nPa7M4
iTunes: http://apple.co/2n1qvVh
Google Play: http://bit.ly/2xwNd1m
B&N: http://bit.ly/2wkBJxM

Covet (Book 2)

US: http://amzn.to/2pIYCqH
UK: http://amzn.to/2pJgimr
CA: http://amzn.to/2oW1PiB
AU: http://amzn.to/2qj61KK
iTunes: http://apple.co/2v4CXrp
B&N: http://bit.ly/2xpaMIu
Kobo: http://bit.ly/2h7NaCf
Google Play: http://bit.ly/2ReumRi

*Covet is NOT a stand-alone. From the Ashes - MUST BE read first in order to understand the storyline.

Keep reading for the prologue...

prologue
skyla

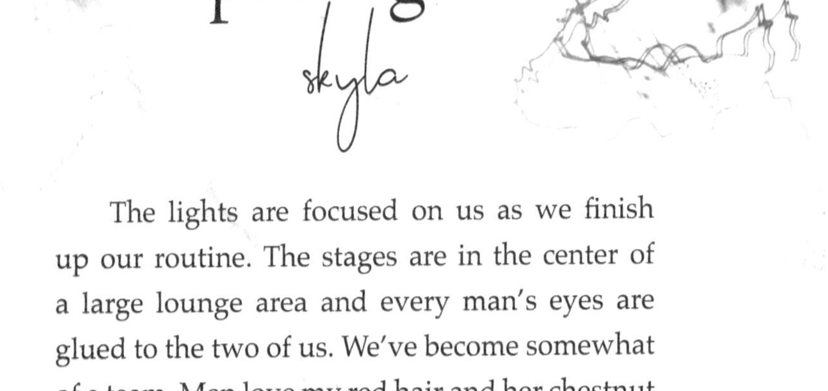

The lights are focused on us as we finish up our routine. The stages are in the center of a large lounge area and every man's eyes are glued to the two of us. We've become somewhat of a team. Men love my red hair and her chestnut locks. Her hazel eyes and my emerald pools seem to hypnotize them.

There are two platforms, mine which is off to the left has one sleek, silver pole, and to the right Dakota's has a chair, which she's currently leaning on as the song ends. Her long, slender legs shimmer with the glitter she brushed on earlier.

Inferno.

The nightclub that's given me a sanctuary from my past. An elite club with only the richest of clientele. They pay an exorbitant fee to see me wrap my legs around a metal pole. They watch me and the girls, sway and gyrate, wearing slinky outfits. They beg us to taunt them.

For the more exclusive clients, there's a menu if they'd like more than just a dance. When they request something from that sleek silver card, we're at their beck and call.

From where I'm positioned backstage, I notice Dax, my boss, and Axel, the head of security—the only two men I trust since leaving the hell I came from—stalking toward the bar. They've been good to me and the other girls who work for them.

"Skyla,"—Dakota's melodic voice drags me from my daydreams of another life—"orders up!" she quips, with a smile so bright it lights up her face. I know what she means, two clients requested us. The VIP package in this place means men can ask for any girl to join them in a private room, and if they pay the premium, they get to fuck us, and it seems tonight Kota—which is her stage name—and I will be entertaining someone.

I follow my best friend down the hallway. "Which room are we in?"

She glances at the card that Theia gave her and responds over her shoulder. "The Raven Room, looks like we have two men to dance for tonight." This room is mine—well, it's my favorite. With muted colors and a beautiful pole in the center, I feel as if they made it for me.

Upon entering we find the clients already seated in the onyx wingback chairs. They're both older, possibly mid-forties. One of them has a thick gold band on his ring finger, glimmering under the low lights coming from the ceiling.

"What can we do for you gentlemen today?" I stop only a few feet from them, my red panties and bra leave little to the imagination. Dakota heads to the pole, twirling around it hypnotically. I've been teaching her some moves and she's picking them up quickly.

"I'm Travis. This is Rich. He wants to watch, doesn't want to cheat on his wife," the one with salt-and-pepper hair says, gesturing to his friend. I almost laugh at that. Of course he doesn't. "I, on the other hand, would love to control you and your little friend," he quips, and I nod in understanding.

"You want a dirty show?" I question, meeting the steel gray eyes of Rich. His dark brown hair is just graying at the sides. He nods. No fucking shame. "Fine, make yourselves comfortable."

Since I've been at Inferno, Dakota's one of the girls I've grown close to, the other is our hostess, Theia. They've both been an incredible support after the horrors I faced. They're both honest to a fault, and love me even in my self-loathing moments.

I think we do that for each other.

After my escape from Caged with the help of Dax, I've gotten attached to my makeshift family. Now, here in the Big Apple, a year into our friendship, we're like sisters.

Dakota's dressed in a skimpy, blue baby doll negligee, which is so short and see through, it's pretty pointless. She might as well be naked. She gives me that sexy little pout that drives her clients crazy. Raising my finger, I crook it to call her over. When I turn back to the men, I find both clients are now shirtless, and for older men, they're toned in all the right places.

Without a word, Dakota heads toward me. Her tits bounce with every step and their eyes are glued to her. "This here is Kota, boys, and I'm Skyla." Two sets of eyes flit between us with eagerness. "Kitten, why don't you show these gentlemen how sweet you can be."

I reach for her arm and tug her against me. My chest against her back. We're standing in front of Travis as I reach for her tits, groping them, tugging and tweaking her pebbled buds.

"Isn't she pretty boys?" Rich is fixated on our display. My one hand travels down her flat stomach to find her bare little pussy. "Open your legs, K," she does and my fingers slip in easily. She's already wet and we've only just begun. I plunge two fingers into her, pumping them in and out. Her soft moans are the only sound in the room, until I hear the hiss of one zipper, then a second.

When I look at our audience, they've both got their dicks in their fists. Rich is smaller and not as thick, but the one who gets to play must easily be ten inches. That's going to hurt like a motherfucker. Pulling my fingers from her, I reach out to Travis. "Taste her," I murmur. He moves quickly, taking my fingers in his mouth and licking the sticky sweet juice from them.

"Fuck, that's delicious." He growls, then rises from the chair with his hungry gaze trained on us and shoves off the rest of his clothes. "I'm taking charge now. You're both going to lie down and obey." We don't argue because he doesn't look like he's joking.

His expression is something akin to someone who just hit the fucking jackpot. With two incredibly beautiful women doing as you wish, no man in his right mind could resist.

"Go sit on her face, pet. I think she needs to get a taste," he orders Dakota in a deep and rough tone. "Toys?" He turns to me, and I gesture to the chest of drawers. I know what he wants and he'll find them all in there. He pulls out the four thick leather cuffs and turns to the bed.

I lie back, watching him gawk as Kota's pert ass wiggles as she climbs on the bed. Rich is in awe staring at us as he strokes himself. She straddles my face and I immediately grip her hips, holding her against my mouth.

My tongue darts out, licking her smooth lips, tasting the sweetness of her honey. The moans that escape her are feral and sexy. The sound of sex is in the air and the scent of K's sweet little cunt has me salivating.

"Enough." The word rumbles between us. Her eyes are glazed as she glares at Travis. I know she was close, wet and primed. "Lie down, sweetheart. We'll make you feel better."

We swap positions, and he goes to work using the cuffs to bind her to the bed. Her legs are spread wide and her arms are locked in place. No escaping now, little one.

She watches me and I offer a wink.

"I need to come, please?" she begs, but he ignores her.

"Soon," I whisper. Her plump lips part with a moan when he tugs on her nipple. Grabbing the ten-inch dildo, he joins us on the bed, and in my peripheral, I notice Rich has moved closer.

"First we're going to devour you." Travis's tone is filled with need. He hands me the clamps and I nod. He doesn't need any motivation. Leaning in, he licks and sucks her sweet flesh.

Her nipples are peaks and I set to work laving and teasing them. Once I've got them both wet, I use the metal clamps—which are attached to a thin metal chain—securing them to each taut bud.

Her soft mewls are evidence that she's aching for her orgasm. I've learned over the year that she's very much a little masochist. She thrives on pain and this has put her in her element. "Oh, please, please?" she pleads, and I almost feel sorry for her, but he's in charge. He reaches for the third clamp from my hand—the one I haven't yet used—and stares at her pretty eyes.

"Now," he orders, and pinches her clit with the metal teeth. Her body convulses and Travis's face is soaked in her release. "Good girl, so fucking sweet." He murmurs and licks every drop she's given him. His cock is rigid between his legs. With a quick glance at me, he commands in a deep tone, "I want you on her face while I fuck her." He grips his cock and I watch him rip the foil packet. "Sit on her face," he growls as he sheaths himself. I shift myself and straddle Dakota's pretty face. "Eat her cunt while I fuck you, little toy." I'm hovering over her mouth, and when her tongue darts out, it sends me spiraling. I grip the headboard and hold myself steady when I feel her sucking my hardened clit into her mouth. The pleasure shoots through my body, igniting my blood with a fire that races through my veins and I'm overcome with lust.

Her body is shoved up every time he thrusts into her, which in turn has my body convulsing without thought and my release detonates, bursting through me as I cry out.

"What a beautiful fucking sight," he

murmurs, in awe of me and my best friend. "Get off her face. We're both going to fuck her." On wobbly legs, I move off Kota, her face glistening with my arousal. He slips out of her and I help untie her. "I want you on your back." He points at me, then turns to her. "You, little doll, will ride that plastic cock while I own your tight ass." Rich is now standing at the bed. His body is tense as his hand moves slowly over his erection.

I lie back, donning the strap-on with Dakota on all fours over me. Her gasp as she sinks down on the dildo is a loud one. It's thick and I know it's filling her almost painfully. Pulling her over me, I watch her face contort as her puckered entrance is invaded by another solid intrusion. "Oh fuck, it's too much." Her whimper is soft and her eyes roll back in her head.

I latch on to her nipple, tugging the clamp with my teeth. I know the chain in turn tugs her clit and her body is now sandwiched between Travis and me. Suddenly, I feel the strap between my legs shifting and a dildo being teased into my pussy. Rich pushes it deeper. It's too much, too soon, when he starts fucking me with it.

We move in a rhythm that has fireworks shooting off behind my eyelids. My body convulses and spasms with the plastic cock inside me. When Travis hisses and spanks Dakota, her cries, his growl, and my own moans send me over and my orgasm grips me, sending me into outer-fucking-space.

ONE CLICK NOW

US: http://amzn.to/2izNLf6
UK: http://amzn.to/2iuqHf7
AU: http://amzn.to/2iGxrGz
CA: http://amzn.to/2iuiWps
iTunes: http://apple.co/2uLpzNG
Kobo: http://bit.ly/2ix4eBl
B&N: http://bit.ly/2h8cPut

stalk me

find me online

My exclusive reader group gets news on all up and coming releases, sales, and a chance at early ARC copy giveaways! Join us, we don't bite… hard ;)

Dani's Deviants

Or sign up for my newsletter and get an exclusive novella not available for purchase anywhere!

Sign Up Now!

also by dani
other reads

Stand Alones

Choosing the Hart

Love Beyond Words

Cuffed

Fragile Innocence

Perfectly Flawed

Black Light: Obsessed

Among Ash and Ember

Within Me (Limited Time)

Cursed in Love (collaboration with Cora Kenborn)

Beautifully Brutal (Cavalieri Della Morte)

Taboo Novellas

Sunshine and the Stalker (collaboration with K Webster)

His Temptation

Austin's Christmas Shortcake

Crime and Punishment (Newsletter Exclusive)
Malignus (Inferno World Novella)
Virulent (collaboration with Yolanda Olson)
Tempting Grayson

Gilded Sovereign Series
Cruel War (Book #1)
Volatile Love (Book #2)

Sins of Seven Series
Kneel (Book #1)
Obey (Book #2)
Indulge (Book #3)
Ruthless (Book #4)
Bound (Book #5)
Envy (Book #6)
Vice (Book #7)

The Taken Series
Stolen
Severed

Four Fathers Series
Kingston

Four Sons Series
Brock

Carina Press Novellas

Pierced Ink

Madd Ink

Broken Series

Broken by Desire

Shattered by Love

The Backstage Series

Callum

Liam

Ryan

Forbidden Series

From the Ashes - A Prequel

Crave (Book #1)

Covet (Book #2)

about dani

author bio

Dani is a *USA Today* bestselling author of a variety of genres, from romantic suspense to dark erotic romance and even BDSM romance. She loves to delve into the raw, emotional journeys her characters venture on, and enjoys the dark, edgy, and sensual scenes that fill the pages of her books. Dani's stories are seductive with a deviant edge with feisty heroines and dominant alphas.

Dani lives in the beautiful city of Cape Town, and is a proud member of the Romance Writer's Organization of South Africa (ROSA) and the Romance Writers of America (RWA). She has a healthy addiction to reading, TV series, music, tattoos, chocolate, and ice cream.

www.danirene.com
info@danirene.com

www.ingramcontent.com/pod-product-compliance
Lightning Source LLC
Chambersburg PA
CBHW021132110726
47900CB00002B/323